The Magicians of Madh

Book I of  MEANDERING MAGICIANS

Read the next books of MEANDERING MAGICIANS by Aditi Krishnakumar

Murder in Melucha
Miracles for the Maharaja

Read more for young adults from Duckbill

The Lies We Tell by Himanjali Sankar
Talking of Muskaan by Himanjali Sankar
Zombiestan by Mainak Dhar
Jobless Clueless Reckless by Revathi Suresh
Facebook Phantom by Suzanne Sangi
The Right Kind of Dog by Adil Jussawalla
Shiva & the Rise of the Shadows by Kanika Dhillon
The Wordkeepers by Jash Sen
Skyserpents by Jash Sen
Daddy Come Lately by Rupa Gulab
Unbroken by Nandhika Nambi
When She Went Away by Andaleeb Wajid
Mirror, Mirror by Andaleeb Wajid
Invisible People by Harsh Mander
When Morning Comes by Arushi Raina
Year of the Weeds by Siddhartha Sarma
Queen of Earth by Devika Rangachari
Queen of Ice by Devika Rangachari
Queen of Fire by Devika Rangachari

The Magicians of Madh

Book I of MEANDERING MAGICIANS

ADITI KRISHNAKUMAR

duckbill

To Amma and Appa, for all the years of the magic that's in books
and the magic that's outside them.

DUCKBILL BOOKS

USA | Canada | UK | Ireland | Australia
New Zealand | India | South Africa | China

Duckbill Books is part of the Penguin Random House group of companies
whose addresses can be found at global.penguinrandomhouse.com

Published by Penguin Random House India Pvt. Ltd
4th Floor, Capital Tower 1, MG Road,
Gurugram 122 002, Haryana, India

Penguin
Random House
India

First published by Duckbill Books India 2018

Text copyright © Aditi Krishnakumar 2018

Aditi Krishnakumar asserts the moral right to be
identified as the author of this work.

ISBN 9789387103054

Typeset in Sitka by PrePSol Enterprises Pvt. Ltd
Printed and bound in India by Repro India Ltd

www.penguin.co.in

PROLOGUE

The streets of Madh, even in the middle of the night, were a beehive of activity.

In any other city of the Free Lands, this would never have been tolerated by the authorities. The odd passer-by or late reveller is one thing. No self-respecting Captain of the Guard wants to look out over his city under a gibbous moon and see alleys and byways bursting with potential troublemakers.

The streets of Madh were a beehive of activity, not because the Guardsmen of Madh were more tolerant than their counterparts in Khand, Sala or Vraja. It was because the multitude thronging those streets in the small hours consisted of not just humans but also Sprites, nagas, daemons, djinn and all manner of spirits from the Realm between Realms. One of the indispensable qualities of a good Captain of the Guard is the ability to know when to enforce discipline and when to retreat into the watchtower and bar the door. Failure to appreciate this difference might turn a noisy but peaceful crowd into a screaming mob of looters.

Every city has a focus, one point around which the tide of life eddies and swirls. In Madh, this focus was the Royal Academy of Science, Magic and the Arts, whose golden domes, despite being shorter than the tops of the buildings surrounding them, dominated the skyline.

It was towards the Academy that two men were weaving their way.

The first, who drew the eye, was clad in a blue robe. He was human—undeniably, earthily human—and imposing. He was nearly a foot taller than everybody else, and proportionately wide. Most of his mass seemed to consist of rippling muscle, though the folds of his blue robe were so bulky that one could only guess.

What people *could* see was that slung over his left shoulder was a great war-bow even taller than he was. A quiver bristling with arrows was strapped to his back.

People made way for the man. Priests made way for him. Guards made way for him. Even djinn made way for him. Once he had passed, people, priests, guards and djinn all looked away.

None of them spotted the grey-robed man padding in his wake.

The men walked past the Academy to Temple Square.

It was called Temple *Square* because that had been the original intent. It was really more of a lopsided dodecagon. Nobody knew why. The temples themselves were marvels of precision engineering. It was inconceivable that a culture that had used sticks and shadows for measurement and maintained a margin of error below half of one tenth of one percent could have failed to draw four straight lines joined at four right angles. Tour guides told romantic stories involving forbidden love, powerful enchantresses, and the sculpture of the six-legged horse on the façade of the Sun Temple. The truth, of course, was far more mundane and far less interesting, and is therefore irrelevant to this story.

The two men picked their way to a small cluster of sculptures in the centre of the Square. The man in grey approached the statue of the God of Watchful Peace, who presided over the revelry with unnerving obsidian eyes.

'Well? We're here.' The man in grey didn't whisper. A whisper would have been conspicuous. He bellowed, and his raised voice was lost in the cacophony of all the other raised voices.

All the same, somebody must have heard, because a moment later, a response issued from somewhere in the region of the elephant on the god's shield. Nobody other than the two men paid it attention; the inhabitants of Madh were as accustomed to strange voices as people in other cities were accustomed to sparrows in the eaves.

'You were to come alone,' said the voice. It should have sounded sinister and foreboding, with a vague overshadow of menace. But it was the sort of unmemorable voice that could have belonged to the assistant under-accountant of a merchant barely breaking even; it only sounded petulant.

The grey-robed man responded accordingly.

'I *am* alone. Chanura is my eyes and ears. And my hands, when I need it. As you may be aware, I no longer involve myself in ... implementation.'

'All right.' There was a pause for thought, before the voice went on, this time achieving a monotone that betrayed no emotion but was still too ordinary to be eerie. 'I have something important that must be done. I know you have a reputation for efficient fieldwork, but I require a high degree of finesse. We can discuss payment after you've understood the nature of the assignment.'

The voice spoke. The men listened. Around them, the crowd thinned as the night turned to morning.

CHAPTER I

Meenakshi had never in her life been anything but perfectly confident. This wasn't due to any particular quirk of character. She had simply never had a reason to doubt herself.

She was sharp—*brilliant*, as her Mathematics Tutor, Alchemy Tutor and Summoning Tutor told each other, and her, every day. She was sensible—*brilliant*, as her History Tutor and Philosophy Tutor never told each other (they hadn't exchanged a civil word since an incident involving two parrots, an Ethical Theory textbook, and a re-enactment of the Battle of Clear Water when they had both been students) but did tell her, often.

Meenakshi would one day be the most powerful sorceress of her generation. It would have been bad form to say this aloud, but everybody knew it.

It was for this last reason that few people, other than her father, her uncle and her foster-brother, could stand to be around her for long.

Meenakshi herself had never understood why she made people nervous. She wasn't cruel and she wasn't unkind. She wished other people well when she bothered to think about them. She put off writing papers and memorising lists of kings and queens as much as the most notorious procrastinator in the Royal Academy. (But when she went to the Academy once in three months to take her tests, she did even better than Clever Raman, who never put anything off and hadn't missed a single lecture since the Great Common Cold Epidemic three years ago. This, naturally, annoyed Clever Raman.)

All of this is important because these were the thoughts that went through Kalban's mind on what he would later describe, with his flair for dramatic storytelling, as that fateful summer afternoon.

Kalban was Meenakshi's foster-brother. His real father was the Prince Regnant of Melucha. His real mother was, while not quite the most powerful sorceress of her generation, close enough to it that everyone in Melucha had heaved a sigh of relief when she had decided that observing goings-on in the opulent luxury of the royal court was more interesting than breeding pigs on her island farm and had accepted the position of the Prince's Chief Counsellor.

From Prince and Counsellor to husband and wife was a short step, made even shorter by the handsomeness and amiability of the Prince and the legendary beauty of the sorceress.

Kalban—his true name wasn't Kalban, but *that* is a story for another day—had come eleven months and four days later. It had soon become clear that he was destined to be neither handsome nor legendary.

Oh, Kalban wasn't ugly or stupid or a wastrel. Far from it. When well-scrubbed by his nurse and dressed in garments supplied by Melucha's most expensive seamstress, he looked as presentable as anybody else at court. He was a competent sorcerer. But 'presentable' and 'competent' were bound to give you an inferiority complex if you grew up with parents like Kalban's. He'd been nine when he'd decided he'd had enough of the sidelong looks and pitying whispers from the ladies and gentlemen of court. He'd commandeered a sloop and sailed out to sea.

If you're thinking that nine-year-old boys with no sailing experience shouldn't commandeer sloops and attempt to take them into the ocean, you're absolutely right. But that, too, is a story for another day. What's important to this story is that, six years later, Kalban lived in the city of Madh, where he was apprenticed to Meenakshi's father, Paras, the Master Sorcerer.

Paras was, without question, the most powerful sorcerer of *his* generation. He was as oblivious to the demands of civilised society as Meenakshi. That was one reason Paras hadn't been appointed Master of the Royal Academy on the retirement of the previous incumbent, an old affront that he resented still and would continue to resent until the end of time.

The other reason was that Paras was Governor of the Southern Provinces of the Kingdom of Pür. Being Governor was a difficult job that left little free time, even if one was the kind of Governor who could, when the First Servant of the Rain God claimed that there would be a drought as a consequence of the Rain Temple not being granted tax exemptions, cause a thunderstorm on the head of the First Servant. While she was at dinner with her family. Indoors.

Kalban thought of all that, especially of the late-night drama that had been caused by a bedraggled, incoherent First Servant standing at the Palace gates in a growing puddle of water, shrieking for the lunatic who held the Governor's staff.

He decided that, all things considered, it was best to go to Meenakshi with his problem.

Maybe 'problem' wasn't the best word for it, though. It wasn't a *problem*. Or, at any rate, it wasn't *Kalban's* problem. It was ... an *occurrence* ... that had occurred in the vicinity of his friend Avi.

Avi, like Kalban, was a native of Melucha and in the last year of his studies. Unlike Kalban, Avi had been in the last year of his studies for considerably more than a year. He also wasn't a runaway or apprenticed to the Master Sorcerer. With the encouragement of his parents, who were more ambitious for him than he was for himself, Avi had joined the Academy at thirteen. He had contrived to achieve passing marks in all his courses without distinguishing himself in any way as a scholar or obtaining his Public Magic Licence.

Kalban sometimes envied Avi his relative normalcy. He himself had never attended regular lessons at the Academy.

Neither had Meenakshi, of course. Meenakshi had never attended regular lessons anywhere. As far as Kalban knew, Meenakshi had never *wanted* to attend regular lessons anywhere. Going to regular lessons meant meeting people and making conversation, both activities that gave her the jitters.

The Royal Academy of Science, Magic and the Arts was the pride of the city and the finest institute of higher education in all the Free Lands. The building itself was sprawling, with gorgeous, intricate architecture decorating its façade. The gold-plated domes shone in the morning sun, the afternoon sun and the evening sun. Sometimes, because of the activities of the people living beneath those domes, they shone when there was no sun at all. The sorcerers and sorceresses who ran the Academy believed in projecting an otherworldly aura.

Inside, the Academy was different to everybody who entered it. Some people saw it as sunlit. Others saw it bathed in moonlight, or pitch dark. Those who believed it bright and airy one moment might feel they'd been plunged into the bowels of the earth in the next. It was rumoured that the spells had been cast before the foundations had been laid; even the original architect, who must have *known* how the building looked, had never seen it.

Avi had been hurrying from Alchemy to Rhetoric (a lesson that the Master of the Academy considered even more important for an apprentice sorcerer than Summoning) and the corridors had been grey stone, slimy and dank as the walls of a prison. This was normal, although unpleasant, and Avi hadn't noticed anything amiss until he'd felt *it*.

Or, perhaps, he had *heard* it. Kalban hadn't understood; by the time Avi had reached that stage of his narrative, he'd lost all coherence. He hadn't *seen* anything; that much seemed certain. He'd heard a voice, or felt a presence, or perhaps both. He'd made a quick decision to skip Rhetoric and consult Kalban. In any case, he hadn't done his homework ('Do you think it is ethical to practise mind control if that is the only way to prevent a battle in which many people may be killed? Present an argument in support of your answer').

Kalban, at first, had been inclined to dismiss Avi's fears. Avi was a good friend of his. That was why Kalban knew that even Avi's good friends had to admit that he was *imaginative*. (His enemies, with greater accuracy, called him a bare-faced liar.) If there were weird lights to be seen, Avi would see them. If there were no weird lights to be seen, Avi would see them anyway, and would throw in eerie creaking noises for good measure.

Something had prevented Kalban from following his usual policy of firm incredulity. When he thought about it on the long walk from the Academy to the Palace, he realised it was because Avi, while always terrified of the bogeys he imagined into existence, also always *enjoyed* his fear. It gave him the only consequence he ever had.

This time, though, there had been none of the subtle delight that coloured Avi's usual stories.

Avi, in the face of Kalban's initial disbelief, had been adamant that he had heard—or possibly felt—*something* malevolent. Kalban had found himself unable to dismiss Avi's story entirely. Of course Avi's stories, while entertaining, were never true, of course he was as inventive as a court-bard embellishing a song with a little danger, of course he *had* to be lying, but ...

But what if he wasn't?

Kalban had rejected the idea of taking Avi to Paras because people who disturbed the Master Sorcerer when he was trying to study his craft found that he wasn't shy of showing his displeasure. Avi might leave the meeting as a centipede or a snail or some other creature that didn't have the ability to knock on doors.

Kalban had heard that Paras, as a boy, had set four angry swans on a classmate who had delayed him on the way to a Summoning lesson with idle debate about the relative merits of magic and philosophy. In most student sorcerers, this would have been attributed to youthful high spirits, but Paras, far from being mellowed by age, had grown more creative.

Paras's brother, Asamanjas, would, Kalban knew, be equally unhelpful. Asamanjas might *want* to help, but he was useless when it came to sorcery.

That left Meenakshi. Kalban had to admit he could do worse. Meenakshi had good instincts for magical residues. If there was or had been something unnatural in the corridor, she would know. If there wasn't anything, she would know, and she would make sure Avi knew not to imagine strange noises another time. (Kalban, reasonably sure she could achieve that without the infliction of any long-term damage, silenced his uneasy conscience with the promise that he would intervene if she looked like using anything stronger than a Level II Curse.)

Besides, as Kalban realised by the time they were at the entrance to the Palace, he was at least partly motivated by the fact that Avi had never met Meenakshi before. It was always entertaining to introduce his foster-sister to new people.

With that happy thought, Kalban led his friend through the Jasmine Garden and across the Pool of Lotuses to Meenakshi's apartments.

Meenakshi was Summoning.

Residents of the Academy had rules about Summoning. In the beginning, there had been only one rule, about Summoning in bedrooms and dormitories. (It had gone on for fifteen pages—Master Sorcerer Vyasa had been nothing if not thorough—but the gist of it could be summed up in *Never do it.*) The students, with typical ingenuity, had necessitated the inclusion of more rules over the years. The fifteen pages had been expanded to two volumes; the places banned for Summoning in the Academy now included bathrooms, studies, corridors, the large dining hall, the small dining hall and the visitors' cloakroom.

Meenakshi, as a resident of the Palace, could Summon where she pleased in her own home.

Kalban had never bothered to object. The possibility of meeting an unexpected yaksha armed with a sword and a foul temper was a far stronger deterrent against unwanted intruders than the guards at the gates.

However, experience had made Kalban careful. He sent Gopali, Meenakshi's senior secretary, to Meenakshi with word of his arrival, and waited in her sitting room with Avi.

It was some time before she emerged from her study. When she did, it was with tendrils of hair escaping from her braids and an expression of such calm satisfaction that Kalban was certain she'd been in conversation with a Class V djinn at the very least.

'Is it gone?' he asked.

She didn't bother to respond, looking at Avi with frank curiosity that made him squirm. Kalban didn't blame him. He had that dispassionate questioning gaze on him at least four times a week. It made him feel like a riddle Meenakshi was trying to solve. It was a disconcerting feeling for young sorcerers-in-training, who were accustomed to being the solvers and not the solvees.

'Meenakshi, this is Avi,' he said, to forestall any tactless question that might be trembling on her lips. 'He's one of my classmates at the Academy. You've heard me speak of him.'

'I suppose I must have done. Why are you here?'

'We're both well, Meenakshi, thank you for asking. How are you?'

Meenakshi rolled her eyes. 'I'm sorry. How are you, Kalban? Did you sleep well? Oh, of *course* you did. I already knew that because you told me at breakfast, and again at lunch. Your friend looks like he hasn't slept for a week.'

Kalban took several deep breaths. He had brought Avi to Meenakshi, after all. He had chosen his foster-sister over the multitude of wiser, more sensible and more experienced practitioners of magic who thronged the city of Madh. And the reason was that Meenakshi, if you were prepared to put up with her maddening combination of genius and cluelessness, was usually willing to help.

Getting to the point at once, he had learnt, worked well. 'We have a problem.'

'What?'

'Avi ...' Kalban trailed off, cringing.

He knew he was going to sound ridiculous. He himself would have laughed if Meenakshi had come to him with a similar problem. He might not have laughed *aloud*, because she could be creative when provoked, but he would have allowed himself a quiet chuckle while her back was turned.

Meenakshi's face grew impatient. Kalban interrupted his own musings to go on. 'Avi heard—*felt*—' No, there was no help for it. 'Perhaps you should explain, Avi. It's your story.'

Avi looked uneasy, but he repeated his story with fewer embellishments than he'd used while telling it to Kalban.

'Well,' Meenakshi said when he was done, 'I suppose we might go and look.' Kalban's surprise must have shown in his expression, because Meenakshi added, 'He isn't the first to complain of strange noises at the Academy this week.'

'Other people have been to see you about this? *Voluntarily?*'

'My secretary Saha has a sister who works there. She heard footsteps following her down the corridor but couldn't see anyone. I wouldn't rely on her word alone; she came to me a month ago insisting that the statue of the God of Watchful Peace had rolled its eyes and shaken its spear, and I *know* the Priests of the Warlords hadn't scheduled any displays. But the Counsellor was in as well. This morning.'

'The Counsellor?'

'Yes.'

'Handles all the things your father is better off not knowing, hasn't left his chambers in daylight in living memory, *that* Counsellor?'

'I don't know any others.'

'Why would he come to *you* instead of going to your father?'

'Why did you come to me instead of going to Father? I expect it was for the same reason.'

'Never mind.' If they'd been alone, Kalban would have asked what the Counsellor had said, but things the Counsellor said were best kept secret, and things best kept secret were best not mentioned in Avi's presence. 'If we're going to the Academy, we should go now. It'll be easier while most of the students are in class. Later on, it'll be impossible to tell between a genuine eerie noise and the extracurricular activities of the Disembodied Voice Society.'

Even with an entourage of four guards slowing them down, it was a short ride to the Academy. Shorter than it should have been. The thought crossed Kalban's mind that traffic in the vicinity of the Academy was thinner than usual, as though people were skirting around it.

Filing that away, he tossed a couple of coppers to the stablehand who ran up for their horses, and followed Meenakshi and Avi into the Hall of the Thousand Pillars.

'Where did you hear the voice?' Meenakshi asked.

'I didn't hear it, precisely,' Avi began, in a tone that Kalban knew from experience was prelude to an explanation lasting a good hour and a half. 'It was more a *feeling*. A feeling of *sound*. In fact, I should describe it as—'

'I don't care how you would describe it,' Kalban snapped. 'Where did it happen?'

Avi scowled, but he turned and led the way.

Kalban followed him through halls that were light and cheerful. Early afternoon sunshine streamed through the gauzy curtains and caught the jewels embedded in the stone carvings.

To most people, it would have been an enchanting sight, but it reminded Kalban too much of his parents' apartments in the Royal Palace of Melucha.

A glance at Avi, unconsciously minding his tread as though the floors were slippery, told him his friend was seeing the mossy dankness of the morning.

He turned to ask Meenakshi what she could see, but before he could say a word, Avi stumbled to a halt. He spun, gaze flitting over the bare walls with an expression that was half terror and half satisfaction. Kalban knew the expression just as well as he knew Avi's storytelling habits, but it was new to Meenakshi.

'What?' she demanded. 'You couldn't have heard your voices *here*. We're nowhere near the Alchemy laboratory or the amphitheatre.'

'Can't you hear them?' Avi hissed. 'Now. Now. Can't you *hear?*'

Kalban exchanged a puzzled glance with Meenakshi. 'I don't hear anything. Are you certain—'

'*Yes!*'

'He's telling the truth,' Meenakshi commented, eyes on Avi in unabashed appraisal. 'Or he thinks he is.'

'I'd say the latter is likelier.'

'Can you definitely hear them?' Meenakshi asked Avi. 'Or do you just feel like you can hear them?'

'I tell you I don't know!' There was distress in Avi's voice— *genuine* distress, not the sort of distress that preceded the invention of more details of the mysterious noises and flickering lights. That was unusual. 'It's more that I *know* I can hear them than that I can hear them. I can't explain it.'

Kalban fought the urge to go outside and borrow a lance from one of the guards to knock some sense into Avi. That was what you got for specialising in Applied Philosophy, instead of Alchemy or Summoning or Healing or even, for that matter, regular Philosophy.

'Do you know where they're coming from?' Meenakshi pressed.

'I can't tell. I *can't tell.*'

His voice rose with panic.

Kalban felt a sudden chill run up his spine. For a fraction of a second, the corridor around him seemed to melt into a whirl of discordant colours before it righted itself again.

He shook himself and turned to Meenakshi, who was looking around with an air of puzzlement.

Before Kalban could say anything, a sudden flash of red light illuminated the corridor. It revealed brick walls and a tiled stone floor suffused with a faint glow from the residual magic that permeated the building. Some said that was the true form of the Academy. Others said it was chosen for the alarm because its burst of normalcy was the quickest way to persuade students to leave the building.

From all around came the sounds of chairs being scraped back, fires being doused and Sprites being Dismissed as the evacuation routine started.

⚜

The ordinariness of the soundless alarm restored Kalban's equanimity. It was a signal that an unauthorised supernatural being had been spotted within the walls. Such alarms were common, and were frequently no more than a Summoning lesson gone wrong. The building was evacuated in any case. It wasn't unknown for djinn or yakshas to escape the control of professors and roam the corridors wreaking havoc until rounded up by the Dangerous Beings Control Squad.

Avi's expression of general terror morphed into one of immediate panic. 'We should go.'

'We should find out what's going on,' Kalban said.

One of his duties as Paras's apprentice (the only condition under which Paras had been willing to have him, because the Master Sorcerer didn't enjoy teaching) was to assist Asamanjas in those aspects of governance that Paras found too tedious (in other words, all aspects of governance other than those involving complex and dangerous spells). An alarm at the Academy would definitely be delegated to him; he might as well get a head start.

'I suppose so,' Meenakshi agreed, more out of curiosity than any sense of duty.

Avi's expression didn't change, but Kalban hustled him back to the Hall of the Thousand Pillars without giving him a chance to object.

The Hall was crowded with students and staff who, with the disdain for danger typical of those who have never faced it, had lingered indoors instead of going to the evacuation point in the courtyard outside. The professors were gathered in small knots, talking in undertones, while the students peered into corners, cast suspicious glances at their fellows, and stalked each other around the thousand pillars.

Kalban evaded the questions of his classmates and the restraining hands of one of his teachers, ducking through the crowd until he spotted the Master of the Royal Academy. He straightened his back and squared his shoulders, trying to look like Kalban-the-Governor's-deputy, who had a right to ask questions and expect answers. Kalban-the-apprentice-sorcerer would be sent about his business, probably with an extra essay to hand in as penalty for wasting the Master's time.

'What happened?' he demanded.

'Kalban?' The Master of the Academy hadn't taken note of the difference in Kalban's posture; he spoke with the same mixture of pity and contempt he used for all students. 'What are you doing here? I didn't know you had a tutorial—you aren't scheduled for more until the Master Sorcerer has spoken to you about ...' He trailed off and then rallied. 'But good, I needed to find you.'

'Until the Master Sorcerer has spoken to me about what?'

'Oh, look, there's your friend ... um ... er ... Swamy, isn't it?'

'Avi,' said Avi coldly. 'I'm in your Advanced Elixirs class.'

'Yes, yes, of course you are. Kalban, is your foster-sister here?'

'Why?' Kalban asked, instantly wary. The mutual dislike between Paras and the Master of the Academy extended to Paras's daughter; the Master never spoke a word to her if he could help it.

'Is she here?'

'She stopped to talk to one of the girls from my Applied Philosophy class,' Avi volunteered.

It was unlike Meenakshi to stop to talk to people, especially the kind of people who took a class under Avi's Professor of Applied Philosophy and didn't make an immediate beeline for the Student Office to drop the course. But when Kalban turned, his foster-sister was, sure enough, in conversation with another girl. Or, to be specific, the other girl was speaking, and while Meenakshi looked uncomfortable, she wasn't actively trying to flee. Perhaps she didn't know how.

'I'll get her.'

When Meenakshi had been rescued from the terrible plight of normal interaction with another human being, Kalban earning himself a rare but fervent smile of gratitude in the process, the Master said, 'Follow me.'

Without waiting for a response, he hurried away in the direction of the dormitories. Kalban and Meenakshi had to run to keep up with the normally sedate, dignified and un-athletic scholar.

They were panting and out of breath by the time they reached a closed door marked with a glowing red star. Several of the staff were clustered there, along with Raman, Satya and a couple of other students Kalban didn't recognise.

The door opened a crack. Kalban tensed, but relaxed again when one of the professors slipped out and shut it behind her. Kalban didn't know her name. She was visiting from beyond the Western Sea to teach Advanced Healing. She seemed to know what she was doing, though. He supposed it was a point in her favour that she was even willing to enter the room, considering that three of the milling teachers were responsible for Summoning and they were all eyeing the door as though it might at any moment explode in a shower of giant scorpions.

'Is this the last of them?' the teacher asked the Master.

'All but Paras. I don't think that's likely. The spike would have been localised to the Palace and she wouldn't have come here at all.'

'Good. Come on, then, you two.'

'Wait,' Kalban snapped, holding up a hand to prevent Meenakshi from going to the door. 'What's inside?'

'Nothing dangerous,' the Master promised. 'You only have to speak to her.'

Kalban would have argued further, but Meenakshi ducked around his arm, went to the door, and opened it. He had little choice but to follow. It was one thing to admit in private that the Master Sorcerer's daughter, being both powerful and criminally heedless, might venture where Kalban dared not tread, and another to be seen in public quivering in a corner while his foster-sister walked into rooms containing supernatural beings.

Standing in a pool of sunlight by the open window was the loveliest woman Kalban had ever seen. Her ethereal beauty made his throat go tight, and he had been brought up in the royal court of Melucha, which specialised in otherworldly allure.

CHAPTER II

Meenakshi might not bury herself in textbooks as her foster-brother did, and she had far better things to do of an evening than read the *Historia Nymphai,* but she knew a Celestial Dancer when she saw one.

She had eyes like stars at twilight, there was a slight shimmer in the air, and Kalban was gawping at her like a half-witted sheep.

Since they were famous for coming down from Heaven—or, as one said in these more enlightened days, crossing over from the Inter-Realm—to discourage evil masterminds from their plans of world domination, Meenakshi couldn't decide whether or not she was *surprised* to see one now. The rule-bound Academy was the last place from which she would have expected danger. On the other hand, something unusual *was* happening within its enchanted walls. The Counsellor had been certain of that. Meenakshi had never known him to be wrong.

But whether it justified intervention from across the Inter-Realm Border, Meenakshi didn't know.

She settled for looking the Dancer over and asking, 'Who are you here for?'

'I can only reveal that to the person concerned.' The Dancer, in turn, studied her with a small smile. 'And it isn't *you*, not this time. You're the one they call Meenakshi, aren't you?'

'What do you mean, *this time?*' Kalban growled. 'And how does her name matter if you're not here for her?'

'It doesn't. We like to keep an eye on potential problems, that's all. She's Code Green just now, and anyway, she wouldn't be *my* job. We have three Class IV Sprites on standby for when she turns evil.' Her gaze turned to Kalban. '*You*, we've been watching for a while. You're Code Yellow. But it's not you, either. I think Rambha may come for you herself.'

'Why don't I get Celestial Dancers?' Meenakshi asked, more out of curiosity than pique. She rather thought she'd prefer Sprites anyway.

'Times are changing.' The Dancer shrugged graceful shoulders. 'You think it's only in the Mortal Realm that people demand equal rights? The Sprites have been agitating for centuries claiming they could overcome mortals' evil tendencies as effectively as any Celestial Dancer.' A light, silvery laugh revealed what she thought of that claim. 'I liked the days when there were rules, you know? Old bearded man practises years of austerity to gain the power to rule the world, young beautiful Dancer brings him back to the light side.' Here she preened and simpered in a manner that made Meenakshi feel ill. 'But then you had Empowerment and there was the Great Sorceress Anasuya—'

'She wasn't evil!'

'No, but she was as powerful as any man had ever been and she studied just as far. Her reaction to the Dancers sent down to reconnoitre was polite disinterest. It was the first time that happened. Humans were evolving. We had no contingency plan. Then of course it became common, and ... Look at you wrinkling your nose. How far would a Celestial Dancer get?' She glanced at Kalban. 'It's not as easy to draw away even those who *are* susceptible, with all the young people studying the Arts and using Illusion to replicate what mortals were never meant to do. That's why we have the Sprites. They're into *psychology*. Apparently, *dancing* isn't enough anymore.' A shake of the head, a sway of the hips. 'You have to find out what people want *subconsciously*.' She uttered the last word as though it were a curse. 'We used to be *artists*. Now we have to be detectives.'

'Why are you here instead of a Sprite, then?'

'You think a few centuries of higher education can outdo millennia of experience? The Sprites can keep their Table of Mortal Wants. All I need is a glance, one glance to know who's on the verge of turning evil.'

'Don't you know that already, if you're here?'

'I'm just one successful conversion away from Class III.' There was sudden wistfulness in her voice. 'In the old days it barely took a century to make the grade, but things have changed and now ...' She sighed. It sounded like the breeze in the jasmine bushes on a summer's night. 'Even Rambha's only had one success this year. It's getting difficult for us.'

That wasn't an answer to her question but Meenakshi felt a stab of sympathy. 'What's your name?'

'Chitralekha. That woman who was just here said you two would be the last. Is that true?'

'The last what?' Kalban demanded.

'The last two up for my inspection. We didn't know, you see.

The sensors in the Inter-Realm have been going off for days, but nobody could pinpoint the individual. The spikes were scattered, too, but the Sprites managed to triangulate a source. I suppose they're useful for some things,' she added grudgingly. 'We get much more accurate output since they took over the sensors.'

'The source was the Academy?'

'That's why I'm here. They've had all the staff and students strong enough to trigger a warning in here to see me. It's none of them. You two were my last hope.'

Meenakshi remembered Clever Raman and some other students waiting outside. But she didn't for a moment believe any of them was likely to have turned evil. The idea was ridiculous. She'd heard enough stories of those who turned dark. Evil was cold and twisted and—

She shivered.

Evil was near.

'You feel it too, don't you?' Chitralekha said at once, eyeing her keenly. 'There's *something* in the air here, something that has no place in the Mortal Realm.'

'What is it?' Kalban asked, in his urgent, protector-of-the-city voice. Meenakshi didn't think he was aware that he had such a voice. It would come in handy when he was Prince Regnant of Melucha.

'You know there's something wrong,' said Chitralekha, addressing Meenakshi. 'I can help, but I need time. I don't have time. They'll send me back now. I'm not a detective, remember?' Her mouth twisted. 'If the sensors don't stop flashing, it'll be a Sprite who comes next.'

'What if we ask you to stay?'

'That won't help. I'm here on official business, not a Summons. I can't interfere with a mortal unless malintent is proved according to the rules and ordinances laid down in the *Inter-Realm Guide to Sorcery, Magic and the Arts.*' Chitralekha shrugged, setting her bracelets jingling. 'After the Meru Incident, they're strict about illegals. I'll have my pass revoked.'

'What if you go and we Summon you again?'

She stared at Kalban. 'You do know it's dangerous to Summon a Celestial Dancer?'

'It would be dangerous for me to Summon a Dancer, yes. I'm judging by the conversation we've had so far that you know something about Meenakshi? You said yourself that you'd have a hard time tempting her. She can Summon you. Good luck trying to make her give up everything she wants and follow you to a hut in the forest.'

'Meenakshi is *here,*' said Meenakshi. 'Just so you know.'

'*Do* you want to follow her to a hut in the forest?'

'Not in the least. I suppose you're right. But how will it help to Summon her? We can't let anyone find out. There'll be a ridiculous fuss. You know how unpleasant the sticklers at the Dangerous Beings Control Squad can be. And unless she meets people—'

'She doesn't have to meet anyone.'

'I do,' Chitralekha interjected. 'Unless I see people face-to-face I can't tell whether they have ill intent.'

'It doesn't matter if you can't tell us yet,' Kalban said. 'You said yourself you have experience. You know things. You can tell us what you know.'

'You want me to play bloodhound for a couple of mortal children? I don't think so.'

'And *you*, I'm guessing, want us to persuade the Dangerous Beings Control Squad to let you roam free until you've done your job? Not a chance. Meenakshi Summons you, or nothing.'

'That'll be nothing, then.'

'Are you sure? You're just one successful conversion away from Class III.' Kalban smiled. 'Think. Just a little bit of effort. You could claim it on your record. Chitralekha, Class III Celestial Dancer. You could choose your own cases. Take on only those requiring skill and finesse. And wouldn't you be entitled to a larger allowance? A larger palace in the Inter-Realm, all manner of exotic birds drinking from your fountains, gold brocade hangings in every room—'

'That's enough.' Chitralekha's eyes were a little wide. 'You're ... *good* at this.'

'I'm from Melucha. We may not have great centres of learning or brilliant architects or world-renowned healers, but we know how to do temptation.' He paused. 'You understand that if you leave Meenakshi's study without permission or do *anything* to threaten any mortal—'

'The Dangerous Beings Control Squad will track me down and send me home with extreme prejudice?'

'No, but you might wish they had. *We* will track you down. I will make detailed notes about everywhere you've been without leave. Then I'll lodge a complaint in triplicate with the Inter-Realm Liaison Bureau.'

Chitralekha shuddered. 'No need to get unpleasant. Why don't you two run along and let me say my goodbyes here?'

Kalban acquiesced and opened the door, letting Meenakshi precede him out of the room.

It was some time before they were permitted to leave the Academy. Two specialised Dismissers from the Dangerous Beings Control Squad had turned up while they'd been speaking to Chitralekha. One went into the room to make certain she was gone and test for magical residues, and the other quizzed the staff and students who had been exposed to her.

'You trust her,' Meenakshi said, once they were outside. It wasn't a question.

'The Dancer? She's given us no reason not to trust her. And she can help us.'

'You think this thing of your friend's is real, don't you? I thought you just wanted me to put fear into him so he wouldn't be such a fool another time. But that isn't it.'

'That *was* it,' Kalban admitted. 'When Avi first came to me—well, he's the sort of person who considers a week without strange noises in his bedroom a wasted week. I thought he was just being himself. But I'm not sure anymore. He does seem worried. You said the Counsellor spoke to you about something similar. And now Chitralekha. I don't know, maybe it's coincidence, but ...'

'But you don't think so.'

'There's a household saying in Melucha,' Kalban said. 'Nothing is coincidence.'

Meenakshi rolled her eyes. In all the time she had known him, Kalban had held the unwavering belief that household sayings from Melucha were an unanswerable argument in every debate. That was, she reflected, probably why he barely scraped passing marks in Rhetoric while he got the top grade in Negotiation.

All the same, this time she agreed with him. Something was rotten in the city of Madh.

They rode in silence through the streets to the Palace. In the courtyard, they gave their horses over to the grooms. The guards, who had been escorting them, went off on other business. Meenakshi and Kalban walked through the Rose Garden, across the delicate footbridge over the Pool of Lotuses, and down the path through the Jasmine Garden that led to Meenakshi's apartments.

At the study door, Kalban said, 'Do you think we should tell your father?'

'He'll get a report about Chitralekha anyway. Do you think it'll help to tell him about Avi?'

'I suppose not. Your father was the one who suggested those griffons to you last month, wasn't he?'

'Are you *still* going on about the griffons? I don't understand you! I read about them. You've been after me for years to read those dusty old volumes by hallucinating historians, and when I do—'

'I wanted you to *read* them. I never imagined you would be so taken with a Yaunic historian's description of dangerous fictional creatures that you would try to bring them to life.'

'They're not dangerous! They only eat birdseed. And fruit.'

'Thank all the gods for that. If you'd managed to create griffons with the appetites of eagle-lions ... And I *know* your father helped you with the spell. Forty griffons in a single night is too much for any one person, even you.'

'Thirty-seven!' Meenakshi almost laughed at the familiar exasperation spreading from Kalban's narrowed eyes to his compressed lips. 'Admit it, you like the griffons. They're useful, unlike the Fifth High Loremaster's phoenix. All *that* does is sit on the upper slopes of the Great Mountain of Ice and mope about how its creator didn't give it a mate. Of course, he should have created a nesting pair—'

'No,' Kalban said firmly, as though he thought Meenakshi intended to finish that remark with, 'And maybe I'll give it a go because the phoenix needs cheering up.'

Which she would not have said.

Absolutely not.

Probably.

But then the phoenix might be happier if it had company.

Meenakshi sometimes had the feeling Kalban said No whenever she spoke simply as a precaution.

A sudden look of horror came over his face. 'Do the griffons breed?'

'How should I know? *Somebody* took them away and put them in the underground vaults instead of letting me study them.'

'They're griffons! They're meant to guard treasure!'

'Just now you were saying they're not meant to exist at all. Send someone to take a census if it bothers you. Anyway,' Meenakshi went on, opening the door, 'that doesn't matter. Do you want to speak to Chitralekha now?'

'Tomorrow, first thing in the morning. I want time to check the records for her activities. We'll know what to expect from her.'

'Have you heard anything about her? What she was like before, I mean?'

'Before the Accord was signed and official record keeping began? Not a thing that I can remember offhand,' Kalban said, smiling broadly. 'And that's good news. We don't want someone who's notorious for luring sailors to their doom or shoving people off cliff faces ... Wait, don't go. There's one last thing. What did the Counsellor tell you?'

'The Counsellor? Oh, that. I expect he'll speak to you about it soon. He's worried about the Academy ... and that professor who takes Applied Philosophy—'

'*That's* why you were speaking to that girl. I thought it was strange.'

'The Counsellor thinks *he's* strange. The professor. I told him it was nothing to worry about because he can't do magic and he said that was the point. And something about how Father and the Master would never notice because they're too involved in research. Still,' Meenakshi added with a shrug, 'being strange isn't a crime.'

'The Counsellor knows that,' Kalban pointed out. But it was no good pursuing the conversation.

CHAPTER III

Meenakshi's spellcasting methods did not, she knew, find favour among the fashionable set.

Trends in the world of sorcery changed so quickly that even *Magicians Monthly* couldn't keep track of them. There was always a new way to project the right aura of mysterious power. One day, it was ravens on writing desks; the next, it was bubbling jars of whatever you could dredge up from the bottom of a pond; and the day after, it might be puffs of red and blue and grey smoke that made people's eyes water and gave them bronchial catarrh.

One thing that had never been a trend, though, was nothing—the no-frills, no-drama, no-extras sorcery that is far more terrifying than any amount of ghostly muttering. That was the kind Meenakshi liked.

Summoning Chitralekha was the work of a minute, requiring a single pentagram and only one candle. It made Kalban grimace—he was the type of sorcerer who spent half his allowance on chalk and incense and candles.

But no-frills Summoning had its advantages, the chief of which was that when Kalban would just have begun drawing his third mandala, Meenakshi had Chitralekha present and standing in the centre of the room.

The Dancer, following an instinct ingrained over centuries of being Summoned, glanced at Meenakshi for permission before stepping out of the pentagram, dragging a chair to the window, and flinging herself into it. The Creeping Vine, which normally took to strangers like the High Priest of the Sun God took to the King's Revenue Collectors (it involved raised voices, guard dogs, and promises of retribution on both sides), slithered over the sill and clung to her like a long-lost friend.

'All right, then,' Chitralekha said, when she'd settled down and petted the Vine. 'Here I am, as promised. Please don't complain to the Inter-Realm Liaison Bureau. I don't want my Mortal Realm Pass suspended. What do you want with me?'

'You can start,' said Kalban, 'by telling us why you were at the Academy.'

Chitralekha, looking bored, rearranged her scarves. 'Why do we usually enter the Mortal Realm? We need to save humanity from itself, nip a problem in the bud, distract a potential evil dictator ... Take your pick.'

'You didn't go after your target, though. You materialised into an empty room and asked for people to be paraded before you. That's not standard practice.'

Chitralekha grimaced. 'Don't tell anyone I told you this. We're not supposed to discuss our business with mortals, especially not mortals on our watchlist.' She cast a sidelong glance at Meenakshi. 'I'll lose my licence and they'll suspend my pass. Your grandchildren's grandchildren will have grandchildren of their own and I'll still be sorting out the paperwork. The truth is,

I don't have a name.'

'They sent you down without a name?' Kalban couldn't keep the scepticism from his tone. 'What's the use of that?'

'It's complicated. The Emerald Alert went off last week. We didn't think much of it, of course. It doesn't take a lot to set off the Emerald Alert. Sometimes we even disable it during Finals Week at the Academy.' The glance she cast at Meenakshi was admiring this time. 'It shrieked for three days straight when you and your father made the griffons.'

'I *knew* it,' muttered Kalban.

'So,' Chitralekha went on, ignoring the interruption, 'the Emerald Alert never went up to Tourmaline. Nobody bothered to check the records at first, but when it didn't go down after a week ... We did think, you know, that it was just *you*. We thought you'd been after another creature a Yaunic traveller made up.'

'Don't give her ideas,' Kalban growled.

'Rambha's surprised you've not tried those aurophilic ants yet.'

'Don't give her ideas.'

Chitralekha shrugged. 'What are you worried about? If the fierce eagle-lions didn't eat everyone in the city, I doubt the ants will.'

'Have you ever seen a swarm of ants? They could eat all the Free Lands.'

'Anyway,' the Dancer said, following what appeared to be her practice of disregarding all remarks that didn't interest her, 'when the Alert didn't go down for six days, Urvashi said we'd better check.' Her tone grew puzzled. 'And there was nothing.'

'No magical spikes?'

'There was a spike in total magical output for the city. And there were individual spikes, of course. There always are. It's term time at the Academy. We were seeing a few students, which is probably why the Sprites triangulated there. But none of those was nearly strong enough to trigger the Alert. There was nothing from anybody powerful enough to be a potential threat.' She glanced at Kalban. '*Your* output's been drying up in the past couple of weeks, I notice. Shouldn't you be getting in some practice before Finals? The Four Elements of Creation aren't going to conjure themselves.'

'I don't understand,' Meenakshi said, saving Kalban from responding. 'The Inter-Realm Security Committee didn't know what was happening, so they sent *you* down to investigate? You said it's the Sprites who do the detective work.'

'I persuaded Rambha to let me handle this. I've been angling for a transfer to the Dangerous Ascetics Department but you need to be Class III for that. Besides, it'll look good on my résumé if I sort this out. Just my luck, I hadn't been to the Academy since the new security system was installed. I didn't know I'd trigger an alarm. And calling in the Dangerous Beings Control Squad? It's like you don't trust us!'

'What *do* you know?' asked Kalban.

'We checked the sensors by location. The spike came from the Academy. We ran a second check on everyone who lives there or has reason to visit, faculty, students, non-teaching staff, local children sneaking in on dares, everyone. There was nothing unusual.'

'An unregistered practitioner?'

'Maybe, but it would be difficult. We've been registering potentials at birth ever since the Meru Accord. And we do a sweep every six months to track down any children we missed.

The spike we registered was too strong for an infant or small child. The individual causing it would need to be an adolescent at the very least. And for anyone to escape detection that long ...' Chitralekha shrugged. 'It's not impossible, but it *is* unlikely.'

'I think ...' Meenakshi trailed off, uncharacteristically hesitant. After a moment, she said, 'You're right. There's something ... different. I can sense it—now that I think about it.'

'What sort of thing?' demanded Kalban.

She surveyed him with a return to her usual self-possession. 'If I knew, I would tell you. It's like no form of magic I've ever seen.'

Kalban pulled Meenakshi aside.

'What do you think of her?' he murmured, jerking his head at Chitralekha.

'She wants to help.'

Kalban knew Meenakshi hadn't had the advantage of spending the formative years of her life in a court where intrigue was a way of life and hidden assassins as numerous as grains of sand on a beach. But that was no excuse. He'd thought he'd been able to impart *some* good sense to her over the years.

'She might be lying,' he said patiently. 'Can you handle her if she's lying?'

'Just so you know,' Chitralekha interrupted, 'Celestial Dancers have preternaturally acute senses. I can hear you just as well as if you were—'

Meenakshi snapped her fingers. Chitralekha's voice was cut off mid-sentence. Kalban glanced at her and saw that her mouth was still moving. She seemed to have no idea she'd gone mute.

'What did you do?'

'Look down,' Meenakshi said.

Kalban did, and found himself a foot above the ground. He yelped and clutched at Meenakshi's arms.

'Calm down. You're fine. I've just sucked out the air in a bubble around us.'

'Oh. Of course.' Kalban released her and straightened. 'I knew that. Sound doesn't travel in a vacuum. Why didn't I think of that?'

'Because you were too busy thinking about spies and turncoats and knives in the dark. I'm not saying there aren't any of the above in the world, or even in the city. But what could *she* gain by lying?'

'We'd let her stay. The Dangerous Beings Control Squad hasn't permitted a Dancer to linger without a definite mark in, I don't know, eighty or ninety years. I think the last time was during your great-grandfather's governorship.'

'What if your crazy friend was telling the truth? If the thing he heard wasn't a figment of his overactive imagination, it must be linked to whatever set off the Inter-Realm Sensors. Chitralekha said they traced the spike to the Academy.'

'Coincidence.'

Even as Kalban said it, he knew the idea was laughable. He himself had told Meenakshi several times that only those who wanted to be assassinated attributed unexplained events to coincidence.

Meenakshi didn't bother with a verbal response. Her expression turned into something reminiscent of the Numeracy Professor lamenting that she wasn't permitted to award a mark below zero even to the most egregious of exam papers. Kalban, who was as weak at mathematics as he was strong at political science, knew it well.

After a moment, he said, 'It isn't that simple. You know the Agreement. They're not supposed to come here without a name, no matter what the sensors do. They're not supposed to come here just to investigate. That's what the Inter-Realm Liaison Bureau is for. She hasn't shown any documentation. She's talking about her Mortal Realms Pass, but have you seen it?'

'All right, what do you think we should do?'

The words 'We should go to your father' hovered on the tip of Kalban's tongue, but he didn't give them utterance.

Handling minor issues related to governance was Kalban's duty. Paras considered anything a minor issue that didn't carry with it the risk of the city and surrounding countryside going up in flames. Even Kalban had to admit that neither a Class II Celestial Dancer nor Avi's probably untrue story posed a serious threat. All he could take to Paras was his suspicion that Chitralekha's Mortal Realms Pass was invalid and she hadn't made full disclosure while filling her border crossing form. He could just see the Master Sorcerer's reaction if his research was disturbed for incomplete paperwork.

'Your uncle may have something to say about it,' Kalban tried at last.

Meenakshi's pursed lips said she knew he was grasping at straws.

Paras's brother, Asamanjas, had been the first child of the family in the past fourteen generations to lack even the faintest trace of magical ability. Having an inkling, from his own situation, of how that must feel, Kalban had at first pitied Asamanjas, but he soon realised the Governor's brother never let it bother him. Asamanjas was wont to point out that it was as well to have someone in the family who had less ability to make it rain indoors and more ability to know when the First Servant of the Rain God was trying to evade her taxes.

Moreover, Asamanjas, responsible for all non-magical aspects of administration, had even less free time than his brother. When it came to magic, and especially when it came to anything that fell under the purview of the Magical Beasts and Beings Act, Asamanjas followed a strict policy of non-interference.

'If we let her go, she'll just come back somewhere else,' Kalban said at last. 'Somewhere without alarms. Or, worse, they'll send Sprites down instead.'

'Maybe that's not such a bad idea.'

Kalban stared at her. 'What do you mean?'

'Nothing.'

Kalban knew that *nothing*. That was the *nothing* you heard before you were licked by an inquisitive tongue in the middle of the night and woke up screaming to find that the Palace was full of wolves the size of mountain bears.

Before he could demand an explanation, the door opened and Gopali, the senior of Meenakshi's secretaries, slipped in. She looked agitated. It was unlikely to be due to Chitralekha's presence. The members of the Palace staff were accustomed to opening doors and encountering unidentified supernatural beings. It had become a way of life for them.

Meenakshi and Kalban exchanged a glance. She snapped her fingers. Kalban stumbled when his feet hit the ground, and then glared at her.

'Try for a softer landing next time!'

'Don't whine. You're fine. What is it, Gopali?'

'You have a visitor,' the young woman said. 'The High Priest of the Sun God requests an audience.'

Kalban doubted that the High Priest of the Sun God had said anything so polite.

'Show him into my sitting room.' Meenakshi turned to Chitralekha. 'You stay here and don't touch *anything*. We'll be back.'

Kalban debated staying with Chitralekha. It seemed unwise to leave her to her own devices. On the other hand, it was even more unwise to let Meenakshi speak to the High Priest of the Sun God unsupervised.

In the end, he followed Meenakshi out the door.

The High Priest of the Sun God was a large, spare man. He had the healthful look of someone who rose at dawn, went to bed at dusk, and filled the intervening time with plenty of vigorous outdoor exercise. This was, in fact, precisely the sort of person he was. Not for him hours spent ringing bells and swinging censers in a fug of incense and sandalwood smoke. The Sun God didn't trace his heavenly path within the stone walls of the Temple, and neither did his High Priest.

Paras couldn't stand the man, partly because Paras couldn't stand anybody, and partly because he had a tendency to turn every City Council meeting into a long debate about lower taxes, more lands for the Sun Temple, lower taxes, discounts and incentives to pilgrims, and lower taxes. Whenever his name came up in discussion around the breakfast table, the word 'charlatan' was bandied about, along with 'fraud', 'nuisance', 'ignorant backwater moron' and 'set the phoenix on'.

The High Priest was looking around the sitting room with undisguised curiosity. Kalban's sitting room, which he had visited in the past, was lavishly supplied with jars of bubbling liquid, joss sticks, mystic talismans and books of arcane spells that had been discredited by modern research.

Meenakshi's, on the other hand, looked like a sitting room, with no extraneous features other than the two concentric circles painted on the floor.

The High Priest was disconcerted. It always throws a man off balance if, entering a room prepared to remain unperturbed by the air of otherworldly danger it possesses, he finds no air of otherworldly danger and is instead settled in a padded armchair and offered a cup of spiced wine. He was disconcerted enough that he didn't even notice he was sitting half inside the Summoning circle.

'My lady,' he said formally to Meenakshi. 'Lord Kalban. I thought I might find you here.'

'Can we help you, High Priest?'

'There's a matter I must discuss with you. I wanted to discuss it with your father, in fact,' he added to Meenakshi, 'but I was told he's left word that anybody who disturbs his work today will have phoenix-feeding duty for the next six months.'

'What is it?' Kalban asked.

'The statue of the God of Watchful Peace is moving.'

Kalban was unimpressed. The statue of the God of Watchful Peace was a fifteen-foot-tall eyesore that occupied the central plinth of Temple Square. Public opinion was divided over whether the sculptor had been drunk or trying to revenge himself on the Priests of the Warlords for cutting his agreed-upon fee in half when he didn't deliver the statue on schedule. Kalban personally inclined to the second of those theories.

Whatever the reason, in a quarter of the city renowned for its fine carvings, delicate scrollwork and soaring columns, the God of Watchful Peace stood out like a crow in a flock of butterflies.

Legend had it that, when danger threatened the city, the god would turn on his plinth and face the direction of the threat. According to records, this had happened twice in the history of Madh: once during the Battle of the Eight Djinn and once during the Meru Incident.

What *did* happen often was the god rolling his eyes and shaking his spear. This was accomplished by means of an ingenious system of levers and pulleys, and tended to happen when the priests were demanding grants of gold, land and cattle, and wanted a clinching argument.

The High Priest saw and correctly interpreted Kalban's expression.

'Not that,' he said quickly. 'We're not doing it, Kalban. None of the priests is doing it. I would know.'

'What's happening? Has the God of Watchful Peace turned towards the south?'

The south was the only direction from which Kalban saw danger. To the north lay the rest of Pür. The Maharaja, motivated by a healthy combination of fear of Paras and friendship for Asamanjas, was unlikely to march on Madh. To the east lay the

Mountains of Ice over which no conquering army could pass, unless it was made of battalions of yeti riding giant mountain goats (Kalban made a mental note never to let that observation reach Meenakshi's ears). To the west lay Melucha and the ocean.

To the south was mile upon mile of barren desert. It was rumoured that on the other side of the desert was something marvellous. Some people said it was the immortal City of the Gods wreathed in eternal spring, others that there was a strange and wonderful kingdom with streets strewn with rubies and fountains brimming with milk and honey and wine, or a land where animals were wise and ancient and spoke in tongues and ruled themselves.

Any of these things, Kalban felt, was a potential threat.

But the High Priest of the Sun God was shaking his head.

'No, it would be easier if that were it. The statue has ... Oh, I can't explain. You'll have to see it for yourself.'

CHAPTER IV

'Is it just my imagination,' Meenakshi said, 'or do too many people in the last two days find themselves unable to explain what they mean?'

By the glance Kalban cast her, she knew he was troubled.

Meenakshi didn't know Avi well, or for that matter, at all, but he had struck her as just the sort of idiot who would imagine things and then emerge severely lacking when it came to finding words to describe them. It said a lot that he was still taking Rhetoric at his age; most people passed all seven levels in their first three years and moved on to Thunderous Declamation.

The High Priest of the Sun God, on the other hand, had a vocabulary that could rival that of any eminent linguist. If he couldn't find words to describe something, it was likely that no words existed.

'I'll go see about the statue,' Kalban said at last. 'You stay here. I don't dare leave Chitralekha by herself. Of the two of us, you're the one who might be able to control her.'

'You're leaving her here? What do I do with her?'

'Keep an eye on her. Make certain she stays here. Talk to her if you can.' Kalban shrugged. 'I know small talk is worse than exam week for you, but I'll be back in a couple of hours. You won't have to pretend to be a civilised person very long.'

Kalban ran off without waiting for her response, probably because he didn't want to have a discussion about it. Meenakshi briefly debated casting a spell to stop him at the door, just on principle, but there were things she had to do as well, things that could be better done without Kalban standing at her shoulder nagging her about caution and good sense and the Inter-Realm Code of Sorcery.

She returned to her study to find Chitralekha waiting exactly where she had left her.

'I sat here,' Chitralekha said at once. 'I didn't touch anything.'

'Good. Keep doing that. Feel free to make small talk.'

'By myself? What are you going to do?'

'Scry.'

There were practitioners who thought scrying had to involve an enchanted mirror (one got an enchanted mirror by taking a normal mirror and paying an artisan a couple of silvers to emboss the first line of the Litany of Time around the edges). While the words were unnecessary, it was always safer to scry through a reflection.

Meenakshi had no time for mirrors, so she took a large blue bowl and filled it with water from the jug on her desk.

'Do you want me to help?' Chitralekha asked hopefully.

'No.'

'I could silver the surface for you. You'd be able to see much more clearly.'

'You can sit there, quietly, until I'm done.'

'You know unauthorised scrying is forbidden under Paragraph IV of Section 87D of the Code of Sorcery?'

'It's Paragraph V.' Meenakshi glanced at Chitralekha. 'Trust me. Kalban quotes it to me at least once a week. Paragraph V.'

'Mortals astonish me.' Chitralekha leaned back in her chair with an air of languor. 'When *we* want to scry, we need permits and licences and about thirty pages of documentation all in the name of protecting your privacy ...'

'Oh, don't worry about that. I'm not scrying a person.'

'What are you scrying, then?'

'The Academy cellars and basements. I could go there and look at them, but that's far too much trouble, don't you think? This is easier.'

'Not an invasion of privacy. Still unauthorised.'

'It's for the greater good. The greater good is better served by my getting on with it than wasting three hours standing in line with the approval form.'

Meenakshi snapped her fingers over the bowl. The water swirled and grew misty. When it cleared, the reflection on the surface showed a long columned room. The walls were grey and unrelieved by any carvings.

'Is that the Academy?' Chitralekha asked, peering over her shoulder.

'The first basement level, commonly used to play forbidden games and hide the evidence of illicit experimental spell casting.'

'Is that what it looks like without the cloaking spell?'

Meenakshi was surprised at the question. She would have thought Chitralekha would know the true form of the Academy. It was an old building. The original spell had been cast long before the Fifth High Loremaster had discovered how to extend the influence of cloaking spells to non-humans.

Nonetheless, she answered. 'I don't think so. I've seen it look like that sometimes. I think it just reflects the scryer in the image as it would in reality.'

'What's that?' Chitralekha asked suddenly. 'Over there ... A little way back, to the left. Can you move it?'

Meenakshi tilted the bowl, letting the flash of movement slide to the centre. Once it was in focus, it expanded. All that was visible on the surface of the water was a blanket of pulsating, migraine-inducing colours—reds and blues and greens and yellows—mixing and glowing and writhing like serpents.

Chitralekha let out an audible gasp. 'That's—that's the other Realm. Our Realm. I didn't know you could scry it.'

'Really? I'm still scrying the Academy. So if that's the other Realm ...' Meenakshi studied the display. It looked nothing like the pictures she had seen, which involved gorgeously attired men and women walking among trees laden with jewel-bright fruit or lounging in halls whose architecture was uncannily Yaunic. 'I thought your Realm was full of white marble and marvellous tapestries and gardens of unearthly blossoms.'

Chitralekha tutted. 'I always said we should have insisted on vetting the Inter-Realm Geography textbooks you use, but everyone else thought it didn't matter. All the art and architecture you've read about is confined to our cities ... There we've tried, and generally managed, to tame Chaos. You can see glimpses of it, like in the fruit on the trees. When it looks so bright you feel like it couldn't have grown naturally, it hasn't. That's Chaos shining through. And outside the cities, where there's only Chaos ... That's like this.'

Meenakshi shook her head. 'Why would there be a portal into Chaos? Even the most determined Dark Seeker knows not to risk it. Does anything live there?'

'Oh, yes. Spirits more powerful and terrible than any mortal could imagine. Unnamed and unpredictable things that even frighten me. But if one of those were loose in Madh, you would know about it. We would know about it; the Inter-Realm Sensors would have blown from the overload. It isn't that.'

Meenakshi would have asked another question, but there was a sudden scream from just outside the window. She straightened, letting the image dissipate. She and Chitralekha both stared in the direction of the sound.

A moment later, the door was flung open and Gopali ran in, followed by Saha, Meenakshi's junior secretary.

'Are you all right?' Saha gasped. 'What happened?'

'There's someone outside the window. It sounded like a man. He probably ran afoul of the Creeping Vine.' Meenakshi made to go and see who it was, but Gopali grabbed her arm and pulled her back.

'No. It might be dangerous. Anyone here for a legitimate purpose would have asked for admittance at the door instead of skulking about the garden and getting caught by the Creeping Vine. The guards will be there in a moment to apprehend the villain.'

'I'll see,' Chitralekha offered.

She went to the window and leaned out. When she turned around, her lips were twitching with amusement.

'It's a large man in a blue ... garment. Not a very helpful garment, if his intention is either modesty or protection from the cold, but then it's a warm morning. He appears to be armed.'

'One of the Free Bows?' Saha shrieked.

'One of the Free Bows,' Meenakshi agreed, smiling. 'I take it the guards have reached him?' she asked Chitralekha, who nodded. 'Good. They'll bring him up.'

The Free Bows had once been called Criminals Anonymous (No Robbery Too Violent). But that name had aroused feelings of mistrust, fear and dislike in their target market. They wanted people to fear them, and they didn't care if people disliked them, but they also wanted people to hire them and pay handsomely for their services, and for that, there had to be trust. They had employed an earnest young woman to rebrand their image. She had conducted several focus groups and a poll on the streets of Madh. Based on the results of this, and after much deliberation, they had renamed themselves the Free Bows, a name that suggested more positive things, like freedom and skill in archery, without undermining their record for precision in murder.

There were two types of Free Bows. The Initiate Free Bows were common cutpurses, thieves and murderers. They could be hired for a modest fee from any Licensed Concierge. The others, who simply called themselves the Free Bows, were shadows of whose existence you weren't aware until your lifeblood was welling onto the ground. Rumour had it that to see the face of a Free Bow was instant death, usually by means of a dagger sharpened to a point fine enough to split a hair. They were so expensive that people saved up for years to get an hour of their time.

It was clear to which group the man who was dragged into Meenakshi's study belonged.

He was built along the lines of the larger type of brick outbuilding. He was, as Chitralekha had said, clad in a fairly useless garment the colour of a bright summer sky. Its only purpose appeared to be to provide a contrast to the dull bronze hilt of the sword that hung at his side. It was unsheathed, with a razor-sharp edge that gleamed in the morning light, suggesting that the man was both very confident and very stupid. An Initiate, then.

He was standing docilely between two of her guards, for which Meenakshi supposed she had the Creeping Vine to thank. Free Bows, even Initiates, were hard to cow, but you couldn't overstate the intimidation potential of a plant that grabbed you by your ankles and then twined inch-thick tendrils lovingly around your throat.

'Should we take him to the Governor, my lady?' asked the guard on the left.

'The Governor has asked not to be disturbed today,' protested Gopali.

The guard surveyed her, unblinking. 'Exactly.'

Meenakshi stifled a laugh. 'There's no need to disturb my father. I'm sure this ... good ... gentleman will be happy to aid the course of justice by telling us his name, followed by the name of the person who hired him. And why he's here.'

'Client confidentiality,' grunted the Free Bow. The words sounded thick, like his tongue was swollen. Maybe he was allergic to the Creeping Vine. Many people were. 'You can't make me tell you a thing.'

'Shall I question him?' Chitralekha asked.

Meenakshi shook her head at the Dancer's blatant angling for verbal permission to Influence. 'I don't think there's any need for drastic measures. We can find out easily enough.' She beckoned one of the guards. 'I'll need you to carry a message for me.' She turned to the other. 'Can you find the court physician and tell him we need a phial of black serum? After that, you'll be taking this one home.'

The guard looked puzzled, but Gopali and Saha beamed.

Twenty minutes later, Meenakshi despatched a large tortoise to the Free Bows' city headquarters, along with a week's worth of fruit, a pamphlet with instructions on the care and feeding of reptiles, a phial of serum in case the allergy persisted, and an assurance that the spell would wear off in four days at most.

Then she sat down to write a note.

When she'd sent it on its way, Chitralekha said, 'That's one of the things your father's been cracking down on. And when he decides to stamp a practice out, it stays stamped.'

'Free Bows breaking into the Palace? I don't think he cares.'

'Of course not Free Bows breaking into the Palace. They usually have better sense than to try. I meant *him*. Did you hear him speak?'

'Many people have an allergic reaction to the Vine,' Meenakshi said, her mind already off the subject of the Initiate. 'He'll be fine.'

There was silence. She looked up a moment later to see Chitralekha staring at her in mute astonishment.

'Powerful enough that we have three Sprites—*three Sprites*—on standby for you, and you have less sense than a goat. What, you thought he was standing here quietly because he was afraid of the Vine? Or of what you might do to him?'

'Why, then?' Meenakshi demanded, irritated.

Chitralekha only looked at her and waited.

It took a few minutes, but Meenakshi connected the dots.

'No,' she said at once. 'It isn't possible.'

'You mean it *shouldn't* be possible. But do you know what else shouldn't be possible? A Free Bow being careless enough to fall into a trap that everybody in the Palace knows is there. The Inter-Realm Sensors going off for a magical disturbance that nobody is causing. A portal into Chaos in the basement of the Academy. Something's wrong here. You know it.'

Meenakshi thought of the letter she'd just sent, and shivered. Something told her that Kalban, wherever he was, was also looking at something that shouldn't be possible.

CHAPTER V

emple Square and all roads leading to it were crowded.

If anything, 'crowd' was too mild a word. It did not begin to describe the sheer volume of people of every mortal and immortal race who had packed themselves in so tightly Kalban was surprised they weren't suffocating. 'Mob' would fit better. Or perhaps, 'By all the gods, look at that ravening horde. Let's go back to the Palace and deal with this later.'

Kalban was about to suggest that very thing when the High Priest said, 'Come.'

The High Priest raised his staff. The diamonds encrusting the head caught the sun and made it sparkle hypnotically. Kalban resolutely turned his eyes away. For all he knew, it *was* hypnotic.

'Good people!' the High Priest shouted, in a voice that somehow carried above even the buzzing of the crowd. 'Let us pass.'

The buzzing turned to shouting, a cacophony of cries in which Kalban could discern too much 'War is coming!' and 'It must be the Eight Djinn again!' for his liking. People might be rational, especially the people of Madh, but throngs were superstitious. If someone started a rumour that the Eight Djinn were attacking, there would be a riot.

Then he realised that, although they were shouting, most of them looked more like children at a fairground than nervous people in the grip of terror. He could even see a few vendors selling peanuts and bags of sweets to small, sticky-faced children.

They hadn't come here because they were worried about the Eight Djinn. They'd come thinking the Disembodied Voice Society was going to put on an impromptu show.

If this was the work of the Disembodied Voice Society, Kalban was going to file so many complaints their heirs seven generations later would still be making monthly visits to the Petty Offences Probation Officer.

'Citizens of Madh!' he called, in a voice honed and strengthened by years of relentless training in Declamation. 'I am here to see this marvel that I may lay it before the wisdom of the Master Sorcerer. Let us pass!'

As he had expected, he made no more impression than the High Priest had done. He stood on the tips of his toes, trying to peer over the heads of the crowd, but he was still too far from Temple Square to see anything but more people.

'Just *come*,' the High Priest said. 'They're not going to move.'

He plunged into the sea of people, dragging Kalban with him. By dint of shouting, pushing and the High Priest jabbing several unfortunate individuals in the toes with his staff, they eventually found themselves in Temple Square at the base of the statue.

As soon as Kalban saw it, he knew that there was plenty wrong.

The statue of the God of Watchful Peace normally towered

several feet over the heads of even the tallest djinn. Today its height had been cut in half: the god had laid down his spear and shield and was sitting cross-legged on his plinth, his usual stern expression replaced by a benign smile.

'You see?' the High Priest hissed in Kalban's ear. 'You wouldn't have believed me if I hadn't shown you.'

'How did you do it?'

'We didn't do it. We *couldn't* do it, Kalban. It's carved out of a single block of marble, other than the arms—all we can do is make him shake his shield and his spear. We can't make him bend his legs or sit. Or smile.'

'Could someone have replaced the statue with another?'

'In the middle of Temple Square? Without being seen?'

'So ... the conclusion is that someone altered the structure of solid marble.'

'Someone.' The High Priest shrugged. 'Some*thing.*'

'When did this happen?'

'It was fine this morning.' The High Priest glanced at the ground. 'Do the Academy crypts extend this far?'

'Oh, yes. But it couldn't ... Well, I suppose it could be that, but I'd be surprised.'

The crypts were at the lowest level of the Academy, a good fifty feet below the ground. As far as Kalban knew, everyone saw them the same way: too-hot, too-humid rooms with damp, mossy stone walls. They were where the detritus of old magic was stored: things too powerful or too cursed or simply too unknown for anybody to risk destroying or keeping in plain view. The founders of the Academy, showing unusual foresight (and unusual insight into what would happen if you put a bunch of adolescents in a building and taught them how to manipulate the laws of Physics), had provided vast crypts that extended under half the city.

But the crypts were shielded as well as anything could be. And there was a groundskeeper's assistant whose job consisted solely of walking through the city every day looking for magical seepage where the shields had worn thin.

'It couldn't be,' Kalban muttered.

'I'll take your word for it. What *could* it be?'

'It's not difficult magic, if you go about it the right way.' Kalban studied the statue. 'Exactly the same size, isn't it?'

'We'd have to get a sculptor in to be certain, but as far as I can tell, yes. It's the same size.'

Kalban nodded. 'It's easy enough, then. To produce stone from thin air, or to make it disappear into thin air, would be complicated, and beyond most students—beyond even most of the professors at the Academy.'

'In other words,' the High Priest said dryly, 'our task would have been far easier, and the people of the city not particularly more perturbed, if the statue had shrunk to half its size.'

Kalban laughed. 'Perhaps. I'll have someone from the Accidental Magic Reversal Unit come by to put it right and check for residues.'

For a moment, Kalban thought the High Priest might smile. He'd never seen the High Priest smile, not even on the occasion two years ago when Asamanjas had grown so tired of conveying his demands to Paras and persuading Paras not to turn the High Priest into a black beetle that he'd quietly made a grant of one thousand acres of prime rice land to the Sun Temple.

But then the High Priest scowled and shook his head. Kalban knew that look. It was the Temples-shouldn't-have-to-pay-taxes look.

The High Priest pulled Kalban aside, into the gatehouse of the Sun Temple. He ordered the guards to go settle the crowd, and turned to Kalban as soon as they had gone.

'No,' the High Priest said. 'That's not enough. I'm sure they can put it right. I'm sure you can put it right. But this shouldn't have happened at all. Temple Square is off limits. Even the youngest children at the Academy know that.'

'If there are residues, we'll be able to trace them.'

'And the child will be punished? I don't want this happening again.'

Kalban responded with a scowl of his own. '*If* it turns out to have been one of the students, the Master of the Academy will take appropriate disciplinary action. That isn't your business. In any case, it's harmless mischief and easily undone.'

'Harmless? You think this is about the statue? I thought you had more sense. This is about them.' He gestured at the crowd, on which the guards had, so far, managed to make no impression. 'This is about thousands of people thinking disaster is coming and panicking.'

'Nobody's panicking. If anything, I'd say they're hoping for some excitement. If someone wants to cause a public panic by producing ill omens, he shouldn't pick a city where people hear entire packs of wolves howling in the night and see red clouds blot out the sun like locusts and tell each other it must be the Auguries and Portents Final. You know that. I know that.'

'That may be,' said the High Priest. 'Under normal circumstances. This time it's different. I don't know why. They're not reacting badly yet, but they're not far from it. It won't take much to set them off.'

Looking around, Kalban had to concede the truth of that. Although, at the moment, most people were enjoying the spectacle, there was undoubtedly an undercurrent of tension.

'The Academy will deal with it,' he said at last. 'If it's someone related to the Academy.'

'I don't suppose ...' the High Priest trailed off.

Kalban suppressed a sigh with difficulty. 'You don't suppose what?'

'I don't suppose your foster-sister did this?'

'No.'

'She has been known to have a ... let's call it a lack of due regard for regulations.'

Kalban had to admit that Meenakshi was capable of ignoring any rule that didn't suit her. She would have told him, though. Maybe not at once, but she would have told him before she let him go off with the High Priest and be caught unawares by a God of Watchful Peace who had abandoned his watchfulness and appeared ready to challenge a cousin to a friendly game of dice.

Besides ...

'No,' Kalban said, more firmly this time. 'This is barely a challenge. She wouldn't do it if you asked her to. If you wake up one day and find the walls of your Temple turned into solid gold, on the other hand, by all means hold Meenakshi to account.'

'I thought that wasn't possible.'

'They say it isn't. That's why Meenakshi might try it.'

'Really?' the High Priest asked, eyes gleaming.

Kalban laughed. 'If you want to try to persuade her, be my guest. That's as good a way of any of verifying the Theory of Elements. But be aware that the Governor *will* raise the wealth tax on the Sun Temple in proportion to the value of the gold.'

⚶

Kalban took the short way back to the Palace. He didn't want to think about what Meenakshi and Chitralekha had been up to in his absence. He didn't know what scared him more: the thought that they might not get along, or the thought that they would.

Barely had he entered the compound, though, than a young attendant accosted him.

'If you please, my lord, the Governor wants to see you in his study. At once.'

Kalban forced himself not to show a visible reaction. The last thing he wanted was to leave an unpredictable Celestial Dancer alone with the even more unpredictable Meenakshi for any longer than he had already done.

All the same, the Master Sorcerer was second to nobody, not even the Maharaja of Pür, in the intricate web of protocol, precedence and hierarchy in the Free Lands. Kalban, on the other hand, was that lowliest of beings, a Sorcerer's Apprentice. The summons couldn't be ignored.

He went.

When he reached Paras's study, he heard raised voices from

inside. And if Kalban could hear voices through the six-inch-thick door, it could mean only one thing: Paras was in the midst of a blazing row with his brother.

With his hand poised to knock, he paused and listened.

Kalban had no scruples about eavesdropping. He'd grown up in the royal court of Melucha, where children started their education with A for Assassin, B for Blackmail. If you didn't want to be overheard, you shouldn't speak loudly enough for everyone in a one-mile radius of the Palace to be able to hear you through half a foot of teak.

Unfortunately, although he could hear both Paras's pleasant baritone and Asamanjas's increasingly shrill protests, it was all too muffled for him to make out words.

Kalban knocked.

There was no response, but something shattered against the inside of the door.

Eh, good enough.

Kalban opened the door.

Paras and Asamanjas were standing by the window.

Paras, in defiance of the archetype of literature and drama which said that the most powerful sorcerer living ought to be a tiny, wizened, unprepossessing man in a ragged cloak, was as prepossessing as they came. He stood taller than Kalban by half a head and had the same disconcertingly intense gaze as his daughter. Most people who met him for the first time thought he was a decoy meant to test their perspicacity and greeted Asamanjas as the Master Sorcerer instead.

Asamanjas, short, plump and balding, looked exactly unimpressive enough that you expected him to start shooting lightning bolts from his fingertips at any moment. If he bore any resemblance to his brother, it was in the sharpness of the dark eyes that marked Kalban's entry.

They stood in mirrored poses, arms crossed and scowling, so it was impossible to judge who had thrown the blue bowl whose shards now lay at Kalban's feet.

Avoiding the sticky green puddle of whatever had been in the bowl—because in Paras's study it wasn't always possible to tell between harmless green ooze and makes-you-sprout-pointed-ears-and-a-tail green ooze—he joined them.

'About time I saw someone sensible in this room,' Asamanjas grumbled.

This was an improvement on his usual greeting to Kalban, which tended to be something along the lines of, 'Oi, shirker!'

All the same, Kalban said, 'I don't want to hear it.'

Asamanjas, despite just claiming to have a high opinion of Kalban's good sense, ignored him. 'The Maharaja! Again!'

'I said I didn't want to hear it!'

'I wrote to the Maharaja just last week,' Paras snapped, paying as little attention to Kalban's words as Asamanjas had done. 'You saw the letter off yourself. What does he want again already?'

Asamanjas's expression of patient suffering would have been funny if Kalban hadn't been torn between anxiety about the summons and worry about what Meenakshi was doing while he was here.

'You would know if you let me finish a sentence. The Inter-Realm Liaison Bureau has been complaining to him about the customs official at the Madh Inter-Realm Border Crossing. One of the demigods was detained for three hours last week and questioned about some Nectar he had in his overnight case.'

'If he was smuggling contraband—'

'He wasn't planning to sell it to anyone! It was for his personal use.'

'Then he should have had a letter from the Divine Physician. No letter, no Nectar. That's been the law for years. And if he has an objection to that, he can file a petition just like everyone else. Now go away. I have to talk to Kalban.'

With a look that implored Kalban to try and persuade Paras to rescind the embargo on magical beverages, Asamanjas left the room.

'Shut the door,' Paras said, 'and sit down.'

CHAPTER VI

Meenakshi knew, of course, that Something was Up. She wasn't quite so disengaged from reality as most people seemed to assume.

It was true she hadn't learnt to check her sandals for venomous creatures every morning as children in Melucha were taught to do. When Kalban had heard that, he had looked like she had admitted to not knowing how to read, and then given her an annotated edition of *The Bestiary of Small Things: One Thousand Animals Less Than an Inch Long that Can Kill You*. Dreary as it had been to read about the Emperor Scorpion (not dangerous to humans) and the Deathstalker Scorpion and the Masquerade Scorpion (apparently a spider in disguise), the lecture that had accompanied the book had been far worse.

In any case, in Meenakshi's view, the court of Melucha could do with a little less political science. Tutors who taught that C was for Cat, Camel, or possibly Canary, wouldn't have to worry about their students putting H for Hemlock in their soup.

However, thanks to her uncle and her foster-brother, she had, over the last three years, learnt enough statecraft to know that anyone who really wanted to do her harm would have the good sense not to hire a Free Bow who would get tangled in the Creeping Vine and sent ignominiously home in a wooden crate with air holes.

'You think that was it?' she asked aloud.

'You know what I do for a living,' said Chitralekha. 'Trust me. If there is a thing that can tempt, seduce, enchant or otherwise distract a mortal, I've used it. Several times. And that was the manner of a man who's been dipping his cup in the Nectar of Immortality.'

'Will he become immortal?'

'A common belief, but no. It's much too powerful for the human body. You saw what's happening to him. That'll get worse. He'll be happy—oh, very happy—and it will seem to him like he's more alive. For a short time.'

'How could he even get any Nectar? There are border controls!'

'And an unauthorised portal to Chaos in the basement of the Royal Academy of Science, Magic and the Arts. If someone could do that undetected right under the nose of the Master of the Academy, what do you think they might be doing further afield?'

'If the Master didn't know ... No. Even if he didn't, a portal would show up on your Inter-Realm Sensors, wouldn't it? And the scanners at the Dangerous Beings Control Squad headquarters.'

'That's true,' Chitralekha admitted. 'It *should* work that way. But nobody mentioned a portal to me. They would have told me before I came down.'

'Do you think that's the spike you've been detecting?'

'I doubt it. A portal isn't complicated enough to show up as a spike in magical output.'

'Something that came through the portal?'

'I don't know. But *you* might. If something's been through that portal, something strong enough to cause the spikes our sensors caught, it would leave magical residues as it came through. You can sense them.'

'I'd have to go there,' Meenakshi protested. 'And before you suggest it, I'm not leaving you here alone.'

'I'll come with you.'

'And set off the alarm again? Why, are you trying to test the Control Squad's response time?'

'You Summoned me this time. I won't set off anything.'

'If someone sees you—'

Chitralekha laughed, twirling in the air. When she became still, her face had ... changed. Meenakshi couldn't put her finger on it; she looked no *different* than she had a moment ago, but she was less unreal somehow. More human.

'Let's go see,' Chitralekha urged. 'That was the reason you went there in the first place. If we go at once, you can even be back in time for lunch.'

'Fine,' Meenakshi said.

Kalban would lecture her, but Kalban wasn't here, and she had long been able to tune out his voice when he started talking like he was her elderly great-uncle. If something *had* wandered in from the Inter-Realm, it was ... better than some of the options that had flitted through her mind when the Counsellor had spoken to her. It was the sort of problem that Kalban could put in the hands of the Dangerous Beings Control Squad while Meenakshi got on with other things.

They left at once, declining her guards' offer to accompany them. They would make better time on foot without a gaggle of sword-bearing men wailing at people to make way for the Governor's daughter.

Meenakshi didn't go to the front entrance this time.

The Academy's river gate opened onto the banks of the Tatini where she made a leisurely loop around Madh. Legend, fostered by the Captain of the City Guard, had it that the banks of the river were patrolled by Tatini herself, the guardian spirit of the water. This allegedly discouraged roving bands of pirates from attempting to storm the city by ship in search of the legendary treasure in its deepest vaults.

Every student who had ever snuck into the Academy through the river gate knew the legend was false. There *was* a river spirit, her name was indeed Tatini, and she did accost anyone attempting to enter the city. But she was far too friendly to make an effective guard. If she had met a pirate, she would have offered to help him set up his battering ram as cheerfully as she helped students smuggle contraband through the river gate.

The professors of the Academy, having once been students themselves, knew better than to trust to Tatini's protection. But the guards they posted at the river gate were only human, and Chitralekha charmed her way past them.

In an attempt to discourage students of magic from using the river gate too often, it opened onto the science wing. Chitralekha was fascinated by the classrooms. Meenakshi had to drag her away when she showed signs of sidling into a lecture hall to listen to a lesson about circles from a visiting Yaunic professor.

'I never had the chance to learn Geometry as a child,' Chitralekha complained. 'Nobody had invented it then. In any case, we have no Mathematics in the Inter-Realm. You might let me find out about it now.'

'We have no time. You can speak to my tutor when he comes tomorrow.'

'Really?'

'No! Keep moving.'

Even hurrying, it took them a good fifteen minutes to get to the central courtyard. As soon as they reached it, they were stopped by a professor Meenakshi vaguely recognised as teaching Applied Philosophy.

'Meenakshi. This is the second time I'm seeing you here in the space of less than a day. You don't have any tests this morning, do you?'

'Oh.' Meenakshi just stopped herself from cursing. Sprites, djinn and whatever else might come through an Inter-Realm portal she was willing to face. Providing a reasonable explanation for her presence to a professor whose classes she didn't take and whom she had never spoken to in her life? That was Kalban's field of expertise. 'Yes. This is my friend.'

'Chitralekha,' supplied Chitralekha, batting her eyelashes at the professor and twirling her braid around one finger.

'Ah.' He looked as though there was not enough air in the courtyard. 'Ah. Hello. I ... My name is ... Hello. My name is ...' He paused and drew in a deep breath. 'My name is Datta. I. You. Hello.'

'It's lovely to meet you,' Chitralekha trilled.

Meenakshi trod on her foot. Hard. 'We have to *go,*' she said.

'Where are you going?'

'To show Chitralekha the Academy.'

She brushed past him, dragging Chitralekha with her—

And stopped short.

'What was that for?' Chitralekha hissed in her ear. 'I was only trying to get us out of it without attracting undue attention.'

'Yes, yes,' Meenakshi said absently, whirling to see Datta still standing where he had been, looking right back at her. There was suspicion in his gaze.

It made no sense.

'Meenakshi?' Chitralekha asked. 'What is it?'

'We should go.'

She turned and went on, pushing Chitralekha ahead of her down the corridor until they came to an empty practice room they could duck into.

'What?' Chitralekha demanded as soon as Meenakshi had shut the door.

'There were residues on him. Very strong residues of powerful magic.'

'What? No. That's not possible.'

'I felt them!'

'And I felt *him*. He's not the one who caused the spike. He isn't strong enough. Not even close. I'd be surprised if he could light a candle!'

'There *were* residues on him,' Meenakshi repeated. 'So if he isn't the cause, then he must have been near it.'

'He might not even have had any idea there was anything. Maybe he can't sense residues. Not everybody can.'

'It might be one of his students.'

'Can you get a list?'

'Kalban can. I think his crazy friend takes one of the classes. We can tell him later. We should go see what's in the basement, or we would have come all this way and braved the river goddess for nothing.'

They went on, through two corridors and down a flight of stairs. This afternoon, the Academy looked austere, with unrelieved whitewashed walls and granite floors so highly polished Meenakshi could see her own reflection as though in a mirror. It made her instinctively watch her tread, though her feet didn't slip when they hit the ground.

She wasn't sure she liked the Academy like this.

As soon as they were in the basement, she could sense the residues. The walls were practically vibrating with them.

'It's here.'

Chitralekha nodded. 'It's strong. Even I can sense it. Can you trace them?'

Meenakshi tried to go back through the residues to find their source, but there was ... nothing. Or everything. She couldn't tell which it was, only that there was nothing to trace.

'They're too diffused. Considering how strong they are, they shouldn't be this blurred already. Unless ...'

'Unless? I don't like the sound of that. Unless what?'

'Kalban once told me there's a legend of a ... a creature, a monstrous beast in Melucha. He said it was only a story and as far as he knew it wasn't true, but ... it could eat magic. Or so the stories claim.'

'Eat magic? How can anything *eat* magic?'

'Much as you eat anything else, I suppose. I didn't ask about the mechanics. Fairy tales aren't meant to make sense. But if it's *not* just a fairy tale ...'

'I've never heard of anything of the sort,' Chitralekha protested.

'Maybe someone heard the legend and decided to make one.'

Chitralekha glared at her. 'Is this your way of confessing that you have something to do with this?'

'*No!* I would never make something like that. I think it's a terrifying idea. And unnatural. How would it even work? You can't destroy energy. It would only make the creature more powerful. That was the point, anyway, according to Kalban. It ate magic and grew stronger, and then it ate all the sorcerers and sorceresses who tried to fight it.'

'If there's something like that here ...'

'We have to find the portal.'

'We can't stay! We know the portal's there.'

'We need to see it. Maybe we'll find out who's doing this. We don't know if such a creature even exists—it probably doesn't. I can't imagine anyone voluntarily making a thing like that. But someone opened a portal.'

'Fine. Quickly.'

Meenakshi led the way to the room where they'd seen the portal in the scrying bowl.

There was nothing there.

Meenakshi drew in a breath. She could sense the magic in the basement, not just residual magic but vibrating and alive. The portal was there. It was still open. She knew it.

Yet there was no sign of it.

'This is—'

'Impossible?' Chitralekha asked.

'We seem to be saying that a lot today,' Meenakshi said. 'I don't like it. If something's happened, then it must be possible.'

'Doesn't the Academy train you to believe six impossible things before breakfast?'

'Only the Philosophy department.' Even as Meenakshi took one last look, she knew she was being ridiculous. She had seen that there was no portal. Only an idiot kept staring around an empty room and expecting things to materialise from the air. 'Let's go. This isn't helping.'

She turned.

Chitralekha seized her wrist and pulled her back.

'What?'

The Dancer pointed.

And there was the portal, where Meenakshi had been about to step. On the other side, Chaos glittered. Meenakshi felt oddly drawn to it, even as the squirming colours made her stomach churn.

Chitralekha's grip on her wrist tightened. 'Don't even think about it. You would never come back.'

'We—we just walked right past that to come in here.'

'Look at it,' hissed Chitralekha.

Meenakshi studied it more closely.

The portal was moving. It was so slow that it was barely discernible, but she could see it when she watched the bottom cross the tiles on the floor.

'Is it ... It's not coming at us.'

'No.' Chitralekha tugged her arm. 'I think it's just moving at random.'

'That's ...'

'Impossible,' Chitralekha finished, pulling at her harder. 'Portals don't move. I don't want to stand about here and discover what other impossible things are going on. Let's go back. You can put this to your father. These things are best dealt with by the Master Sorcerer.'

CHAPTER VII

Once Kalban had taken his seat, Paras sat as well. That was a good sign. If he intended to be volubly displeased, he preferred to stay standing and look down on his listener from on high.

'I heard from your brother,' Paras said.

It took Kalban a moment to remember whom he meant. He had a younger brother. They acknowledged each other's existence through perhaps two letters a year. It wasn't that they didn't get on. They had never had an argument that Kalban could remember. It was that, even when Kalban had lived in his father's palace, he and his brother had been a pair of polite strangers, passing each other the butter and making idle small talk.

'From Melucha?' he asked, trying to hide the surprise in his voice, and, by Paras's expression, failing utterly.

'Your parents are concerned. He tells me they have not heard from you for some time.'

Kalban doubted that his parents were worried about him. His father had never been the type to worry much about anything and anyone who was not immediately before him. He had no doubt that his mother scryed him whenever she could.

'What did he say?'

'He wanted to know when you might be completing your training.' Paras shrugged. 'I wouldn't discuss something like that with him, of course. You're of age; it's your own business whether or not you want to tell your parents that you were within a millimetre of failing Lower Astrology. I think, though, that it's time we spoke about your Tests.'

Kalban, who had stopped paying attention after the first sentence, hadn't expected that conclusion. For a few moments, he was too stunned to speak. Paras had clearly meant Tests-with-a-capital-T, meaning the Tests that would declare Kalban a full-fledged sorcerer, as opposed to tests, which only allowed him to proceed to the next level of his training and take more tests.

'You're fifteen,' Paras went on. 'I think it's time.'

'But,' Kalban began. Then he stopped, because he realised he didn't have a single valid objection other than the fact that the idea of taking his Tests—the idea of *passing* his Tests—filled him with nameless dread. He looked at Paras intently, willing the Master Sorcerer to understand. 'I'm not ready.'

The Master Sorcerer, in typical fashion, didn't even attempt to understand. 'Of course you are,' he said.

'But,' Kalban tried again, and again he stopped, helpless.

'But what?' Paras prompted. 'Don't you want to take them?'

Kalban thought he preferred it when his master was obtuse.

'I do,' he said. 'Well, I do in *principle*. But not now. I'm not ... I can't. I don't ... know enough about magic.'

He brought out the last statement with an air of triumph, certain that it was an unassailable argument. Nobody could expect him to take his Tests if he wasn't through with his training.

He was, of course, mistaken. Paras cocked his head and studied Kalban with a knowing gaze that reminded him why, despite being as lacking in social skills as his daughter, Paras was widely regarded as the greatest sorcerer living.

'You're quite right,' he agreed. 'You *don't* know enough about magic. Nobody knows enough about magic. Nobody ever will. It's the ones who *do* think they know enough who'll never be ready to take any Tests.'

There was only one thing to say. Kalban said it.

'When do you want me to take them?'

His voice was laden with the weight of doom. It jarred him when Paras's answer came in a brisk, matter-of-fact tone.

'In a couple of months, I thought. That'll give you time to prepare.'

Two months.

Two *months*.

Kalban felt as though the ground was being pulled out from under him. He hated it. Like the feeling of meeting Meenakshi for the first time, it was something a sorcerer was supposed to inflict, not have inflicted upon him.

Two months was nothing. And everything. It was enough time to prepare. It was enough time for something to happen to prevent Kalban's having to take his Tests.

He bowed himself out of the room.

'Sort things out with the Inter-Realm Liaison Bureau,' Paras called after him as he left. 'I wouldn't put it past Asamanjas to send them in here just to make things difficult for me when I'm trying to concentrate.'

Kalban left the Master Sorcerer's study thinking furiously.

It wasn't that he objected to being a full-fledged sorcerer. He needed to pass his Tests to get his Public Magic Licence, and he needed his licence. Madh's open and liberal policy with respect to magic in the streets was unique in the Free Lands. In all other cities, including Melucha, things were different.

In the old days, of course, the heir to the throne would have practised magic anywhere he wanted, Licence or no Licence (it was usually no Licence), and anyone who'd objected would have been banished—or worse, if the heir was one whose name was later to be joined with words like 'the Terrible' or 'the Cruel'.

Now, though ... Ever since the trouble in Vraja a couple of centuries ago, people were far more willing to stand for their rights, prime among them the Right to Violently Murder Our Prince. If you didn't want to end with citizens dancing tribal dances around a pike with your head on it, you had to move with the times.

So, really, not wanting to be a sorcerer had nothing to do with it.

The truth was that, once Kalban passed his Tests, he would be out of excuses to stay in Madh. The reasons he had run away from home were as valid now as they had been six years ago. Madh, despite the numerous complications in the shapes of High Priests, Celestial Dancers and foster-sisters with more power than sense, made for an enjoyable living situation. But now that he was of age, he had responsibilities in the land of his birth. Only being Paras' apprentice stood between him and being carted back to Melucha to take his rightful place.

His reprieve was about to end.

A glance at the water clock in the Jasmine Garden told him there was no point going to find Meenakshi. It was almost time for lunch.

He reached the dining room just as the Palace bell pealed its midday summons. He settled into his chair to wait.

Gathering in the dining room for meals was Asamanjas's idea. He enforced it with the same thoroughness with which he reviewed the Auguries, Portents and Omens Approval Desk reports. Kalban knew him too well to think he did it out of any belief in old sayings about the benefits of a family eating together. He wanted the opportunity to lecture Paras and Meenakshi on Not Attempting Arcane Spells that Will Give the Maharaja Indigestion.

Meenakshi was the first to arrive. Kalban caught her arm before she could sit.

'Chitralekha,' he whispered, one eye on the door. 'Where is she?'

'Safe.' Meenakshi pulled her arm away. 'I *do* have more sense than you give me credit for. She's in my study under orders.'

'Go nowhere, do nothing, say nothing, harm no one?'

'Yes.'

'You made eye contact when you issued the orders?'

Meenakshi huffed a put-upon sigh. 'Yes!'

'Good.'

'There is something you should know, though.'

Kalban choked on air. The last time Meenakshi had said those words to him, he had spent the rest of the day adjudicating a dispute between two Sprites, a djinn and Asamanjas's favourite horse. And if that sounded like it should be the beginning of a bad joke, well, it had been bad but not in the least funny.

Before he could demand an explanation, the door opened again. By common consent, they both fell silent.

Paras and Asamanjas came in together. Paras's expression was the same cross between mutinous and resentful that you would expect from a small boy who had had his bow and arrow taken away after breaking his mother's favourite vase. Kalban judged that he had spent three-quarters of the walk being harangued on the subject of the Madh Inter-Realm Border Crossing.

As he sat down, Asamanjas ignored both Paras and Kalban, and turned his attention instead to his niece.

'Have you been doing anything interesting today?'

Kalban jumped in before Meenakshi could respond. She was truthful, but her version of reality didn't necessarily coincide with what anybody else thought, especially when she was asked to make relative judgements involving concepts like 'interesting', 'sensible' and 'possible'.

'Did you hear about the alarm at the Academy yesterday?'

'I did,' Asamanjas said dismissively. 'A Sprite or Dancer or something, wasn't it? The Master sent the usual notice. Why, was it anything to worry about? He said you were there.'

'A Dancer,' said Kalban. 'She couldn't pinpoint a target, though. Probably a false alarm.'

Asamanjas shrugged. 'A false alarm. *Someone* trying to invent a spell to turn gold into dross. Something of the sort, no doubt.'

'*Once,*' Paras muttered, poking at his plate. 'Once I set off a false alarm—'

'You've set off *eight* false alarms so far this year, over three visits to the Academy. But, yes, let's call it once.' Ignoring his brother's glare, Asamanjas glanced at Meenakshi. 'I heard you had a visitor in your study this morning.'

It was only by dint of superhuman effort that Kalban managed not to choke. Asamanjas couldn't know—there was no way—

'You should have left him to the guards,' Asamanjas went on, blithely ignorant of how close Kalban had come to dying ignominiously of Being Surprised at Table. 'We employ them for a reason, you know, Meenakshi.'

'Wait,' Kalban said, his mind catching up with what Asamanjas had revealed. '*Him?* Who was in your study?'

'One of the Free Bow Initiates,' said Meenakshi. 'Why do you sound surprised?'

'There was a Free Bow in your study?' Paras asked, a frown beginning to crease his brow. 'What happened?'

'I turned him into a tortoise.'

Paras smiled. 'Good girl.' Then he shook his head. 'I would choose something like a mouse or a beetle next time. It frightens them more. All the same, well done. Standard animal transformation spell?'

'With a two-point time modification. It'll wear off in a few days. Four, I expect, given his body mass as a human.'

'Perfect. Enough time to think about how wrong it is to enter other people's homes uninvited, but not so much that he'll be entitled to file a complaint for wrongful transmogrification.'

'That's what I thought.'

'Sensible of you.'

Asamanjas's jaw had been steadily dropping as this conversation went on. He took advantage of the lull now to say, 'Sensible? That's all you have to say? *Sensible?*'

'You think she should have used the four-point time modification instead? That's overkill for a reptile. It would be too unstable. You don't want to risk being off by more than a few hours.'

'I think there was a hired assassin—'

Paras scoffed.

'Very well, there was an *incompetent* hired assassin who managed to slip past the Palace Guard. How far did he get, Meenakshi?'

'The Creeping Vine tried to strangle him.'

'The Creeping Vine tried to strangle him,' Asamanjas repeated, waving his arms and nearly knocking over Paras's cup. 'The *Creeping Vine,* which grows by Meenakshi's windows. If it were up to the guards, guards whom we pay *handsomely,* a full company of Free Bows could march right in and start attacking us with hatchets.'

'We could turn *them* into mice,' Meenakshi said brightly.

Paras shook his head. 'Use some imagination. We could turn half into mice and the other half into cats.'

'That isn't the point!' Asamanjas looked from his brother to his niece in exasperation. 'There was a Free Bow inside the Palace walls. There are not supposed to be Free Bows inside the Palace walls. If someone is sending them in, I want to know who. I want to know why. I've been having delegations of traders come in to complain to me all morning. Something strange is going on.'

'With the traders?' Kalban asked warily. He had had enough strange goings-on to last him his next six lifetimes.

'No fewer than a dozen of them woke up this morning and came downstairs to find their stock of sale goods transformed into solid twenty-eight carat djinn gold.'

Kalban winced. Djinn gold was a dangerous substance. It had the texture and colour of normal gold, but it shone with an inner radiance that made it impossible to mistake for earthly gold. It was legal tender in the Inter-Realm, because, despite its name, djinn couldn't make it. Only practitioners of magic could.

In the Mortal Realm, djinn gold would last twenty-four hours before it disintegrated into a fine powder.

'What else would it turn into?' Meenakshi asked, disrupting Kalban's train of thought. 'You can't turn things into normal gold until someone figures out how to break the Elemental Barrier.'

'I rather think,' Asamanjas said, 'that the traders' opinion was that their goods shouldn't have turned into anything.'

'Do you know,' Paras put in, 'I believe there's a Yaunic legend about a king who could turn things into gold by touching them.'

'What happened to him?' asked Meenakshi.

'I don't remember. I suppose he came to a bad end. In stories involving kings and gold, *someone* always comes to a bad end.'

'Never mind that,' said Asamanjas. 'Meenakshi—and this goes for you as well, Paras—if anyone enters the Palace without authorisation, I want to hear what they have to say for themselves before you go turning them into tortoises.'

'Mice,' corrected Paras. 'It's always best to turn them into mice.'

'Of course it is.'

CHAPTER VIII

'You didn't want me to tell Father and Uncle Asamanjas about Chitralekha,' Meenakshi said as she and Kalban strolled through the Jasmine Garden on their way back to her apartments.

'I didn't think it was necessary.'

Meenakshi wondered if it was worth the trouble of asking for a reason. Kalban's reasons for doing things seldom made sense to her. She said, 'You might change your mind when you know everything.'

Kalban shot her a glance of mingled curiosity and apprehension. She could tell he was bursting to ask, but apparently years of boyhood training in the royal court of Melucha trumped somewhat fewer years' practice of seizing every opportunity to lecture Meenakshi. He said nothing until they had reached her study and found Chitralekha sitting where Meenakshi had left her.

'I went nowhere,' Chitralekha said as soon as she saw them. 'I did nothing. I spoke to nobody. I think your secretaries must think I'm mute. One of them came in with lunch and I had to use sign language to explain that I cannot stomach mortal foods.'

'Did she understand you?' asked Meenakshi.

Chitralekha considered that. Then she said, 'I think your secretaries must think I'm an idiot.'

'They wouldn't be far wrong,' muttered Kalban. 'All right, both of you—what happened this morning? Is there anything, *anything* at all, that I should know?'

'In point of fact, there's quite a lot that you should know.'

Meenakshi described the events of the morning as quickly as she could. It wasn't very quickly. Her attempts to go directly to important issues kept being interrupted by Kalban asking questions like, 'Which professor was it again?' and, 'Are you *sure* you saw nobody else in the basement?'

'You're right,' he said when Meenakshi had finished. 'That does complicate things. We should find out what Datta was doing before you met him. But he couldn't have opened the portal. He can't do magic that strong. Very few people can.'

'The Head of your Inter-Realm Liaison Bureau has motive *and* she's just powerful enough to do it,' offered Chitralekha. 'If she's anything like ours, she hates the designated border crossings.'

'Nalini *is* always complaining about harassment by customs officials,' Kalban agreed. 'All the same ... I don't like her much, but I don't see her opening a secret basement portal in the Academy. Skulking isn't her style. If she were going to do it, she'd do right in front of her office and in all likelihood she'd invite the Master Sorcerer to the grand opening.'

'There's this Counsellor of yours,' said Chitralekha. 'I don't have intelligence about him—we don't track non-practitioners.

But he could have persuaded someone to help him. He knows everything that happens in Madh, so he must have blackmail material on everyone in the city.'

'You're right,' said Kalban thoughtfully. 'As you said, he knows everything ... So how can this be happening without his knowledge? I've never quite trusted the man. He may have a grudge against the Governor ...'

Meenakshi looked at them with the sort of mild amusement that was the reason she infuriated everyone she met. 'I thought it was only in Melucha that children were trained to see nefarious intentions in everybody. Don't tell me the Inter-Realm is the same.'

'Of course it's not the same,' said Chitralekha. 'Melucha's courtiers write books about poisons and what type of sleeve conceals what type of dagger, but they're terribly inefficient in practice. We, on the other hand, have had thousands of years to perfect our abilities. I take it you don't think the Counsellor is responsible, then.'

'If you're coming up with people who dislike my father, what about the Master of the Academy? He thinks he's the most important person in the city and he and Father have been sworn enemies for years. Nobody would notice residues of magic on him. Why are we guessing, anyway?' She looked at Chitralekha. 'Didn't you say all you needed was one glance to know who's on the verge of turning evil?'

Chitralekha shrugged her elegant shoulders. 'I did. I spoke to everyone with enough power to cause the spike, remember? That'll be everyone with enough power to open the portal. I didn't sense anything ... well, let's say I didn't sense anything I didn't expect. Everyone has problems. So either somebody has suddenly learnt to hide their thoughts from a Dancer—

something nobody has ever done, not even the Loremasters—or we're missing something.'

'There's more,' said Kalban, while Meenakshi thought that over. 'You haven't heard about my morning yet—though I would have thought it'd be palace gossip by now.'

'What did the High Priest want to show you?' asked Meenakshi. 'Was the God of Watchful Peace shaking his spear again?'

'The God of Watchful Peace has thrown down his spear and is sitting on his plinth in the lotus position smiling on all the world.'

Kalban looked grim, though Meenakshi couldn't understand why. 'Someone must have done it as a joke.'

'I agree someone must have done it,' Kalban said. 'Perhaps they even did it for a joke, although I doubt that. I wish I knew who *could* have done it—oh, as far as that goes, I know it's not *complicated*. But most people would have needed physical proximity to the statue. Temple Square's never empty. The High Priest claims his guards saw nothing and nobody.'

'They might not even have noticed. All those people going up and down, what would they know if someone lingering by the statue is a holy pilgrim or an impious student?'

'You think so? Someone must have seen *something*. I wish I knew who ...'

'I didn't do it,' Meenakshi said. When Kalban began sentences with 'I wish I knew', they usually ended in an accusation.

This time, though, he shook his head. 'I know you didn't. I want to know who did.'

'Someone might have done it from below.'

'A student? Temple Square's off limits, and it's not the kind of off limits that's meant more as a gentle suggestion than an actual rule. Everyone knows that.'

'You don't want to go to Father.' Kalban looked mulish. Arguing the point would only waste time. 'Fine. Then I think I know who can help us.'

Kalban looked like he didn't want to ask. Nonetheless, he asked. 'Who?'

'The Counsellor. We can go speak to him. Chitralekha can carry on her investigations.'

'Unsupervised?' Kalban squeaked. One would have thought from his tone that Meenakshi had suggested letting a griffon loose among the poultry.

'You do realise the griffons aren't vicious?' she asked. Kalban looked bewildered, so she went on, 'It's like letting a kitten loose among balls of wool. The balls will scatter and it'll take forever to roll them all up again, but there's no real harm done ... Unless the kitten accidentally claws someone, so perhaps that isn't the best analogy.'

'Meenakshi, normally this surreal feeling I get of having missed half the conversation is part of the charm of talking to you. But I don't have time to unravel your thoughts now. What are you speaking about?'

'What's Chitralekha going to do? If she tries anything, we'll tell the Dangerous Beings Control Squad. They'll have her Inter-Realm Pass revoked before she can say, "Disobeying my Summoner." Besides, she's used to investigating mysterious magical events. It's what they do.'

'Thank you,' Chitralekha said with asperity.

'Fine,' conceded Kalban. 'But not here.' He looked at Chitralekha.

'Go back. Check your sensors—and your records. We need to know if anything like this has happened before. It'll be helpful if you can find out about the Portal, too.'

'And how do I come back? If I cross without a Summons, I'll be dealing with the Dangerous Beings Control Squad again. I can't afford more order marks on my Pass. They'll demote me to Class I.'

'Meenakshi can Summon you again in the morning. Will that give you enough time?'

Chitralekha shrugged. 'Time's fluid between the Realms. You go ahead. I'll find out what I can. Urvashi might know something. She's always hinting that she's seen more than any of the other Dancers, even Rambha.' She brightened. 'If I go discuss this with Urvashi, do you think it'll count as Initiative? They claimed on my last Centennial Review that I wasn't showing enough of it.'

'I'm sure it will.'

Chitralekha vanished, muttering something about a Commendation as Meenakshi Dismissed her.

Meenakshi and Kalban went to the Houses of Governance.

The Counsellor wasn't a believer in first impressions. His offices consisted of three rooms, which, although sunlit (which was itself an offence against all that was fitting; everyone agreed that one who did the work of a spymaster ought to do it in the dark), appeared diminutive beside the sprawling bulk of the headquarters of the Inter-Realm Liaison Bureau.

The Counsellor himself was as cheerful as he was (allegedly) dangerous. It was said that he had begun his career as a Free Bow, and, rising rapidly through the ranks, had been on the point of being named the youngest First Bow in their history when he had inexplicably hung up his weapons and chosen a new and far more exciting line of work.

Meenakshi didn't have the slightest difficulty in believing that the Counsellor had once been a hired assassin. There was something a little inhuman about his cheer. He might smilingly offer you spiced tea, enquire about your family, and then, without the slightest variation in his tone of warm sympathy, merrily plunge a dagger into your back when you unwarily bent to retrieve a letter that he dropped while handing you.

The Counsellor insisted he hadn't killed anyone in years. Meenakshi had asked.

In the outer room sat a young woman who seemed far more intent on studying her own reflection in the polished marble walls than asking after their business. Her self-absorption was, like everything else in these offices, deceptive. Meenakshi knew she had no fewer than eight daggers and a vial of poison concealed about her person. She'd asked the Counsellor that too.

It was incredible what the Counsellor was willing to say if you asked him. It was probably the novelty of being asked direct questions that amused him. Most people who saw him coming down the street suddenly remembered an urgent appointment three miles away.

Meenakshi and Kalban passed through the outer room to a small hall. Twelve young men and women were hard at work poring over maps, scrolls and intercepted secret communications. Other than the occasional murmured request to pass the ink, they made no noise.

They were the Counsellor's apprentices, hand-picked from every family in the land—or *nearly* every family. His only condition was that he would accept nobody who could practice magic. He had his own code of honour: if people were fool enough to have private conversations near open windows, grates, doors, trees, bushes or curtains, they deserved to be overheard, but it was unsporting to watch someone sitting five miles away in a bowl of water.

None of the apprentices gave Meenakshi and Kalban a second glance.

'We're here far too often,' Kalban muttered.

Meenakshi knocked on the plain wooden door, marked by nothing, that led to the Counsellor's private office.

The Counsellor must have had a name. But, whatever it was, it hadn't been used in public in so many years that even those who had once known it had forgotten it. (Those who hadn't forgotten it willingly had done so at the point of a sword.) Now everyone just called him Counsellor.

He greeted Meenakshi with a smile that was three-quarters genuine, because from the moment of their first meeting they had understood each other, and one-quarter cautious, because the Counsellor was always cautious.

'Is it the alarm at the Academy or the God of Watchful Peace you're here about?' he asked.

'How did you hear about that?' demanded Kalban. 'There's no reason to believe it was anything other than a routine false alarm.'

'And yet here you are on the day after the alarm sounded. Meenakshi didn't say anything about needing my help when I last spoke to her yesterday ... before the alarm.'

The Counsellor smiled again. This time, it was entirely fake. Kalban tried to scowl, but the effect was ruined by the fact that he was at the same time placing himself behind Meenakshi.

'What?' he hissed, in response to her rolled eyes. 'He likes you.'

'I might ask,' the Counsellor went on, 'what the two of you were doing at the Academy yesterday, when neither of you had an exam or a tutorial? It's best if nobody displays vulgar curiosity, don't you think?' He turned to Meenakshi. 'I don't know what you expect me to do for you. I suppose the Dancer's appearance might be related to the drama at Temple Square, but neither is my province. I deal in people, not magic.'

'There's a person involved. Somebody's casting the spells.'

'Self-generating magic?' asked the Counsellor.

'No. I would have known.'

'I'll take your word for it. You'll have to help me, then. What happened at the Academy?'

With a deep breath, Kalban launched into the story.

The Counsellor listened without comment, and, when Kalban had finished, shook his head. 'You're saying you think it's all connected? Chitralekha's appearance, what your friend Avi heard, the portal in the Academy basement, the God of Watchful Peace?'

'And the djinn gold and the possibly drug-addled Initiate in the Palace. Yes. I don't know how far we should believe Avi, though,' Kalban admitted. 'I heard nothing when I went to check. Neither did Meenakshi. Avi's been known to be economical with the truth in the interest of a good narrative.'

'It's a common failing. But let's assume for the moment that he's telling the truth. He's not the only one who's reported strange noises in the vicinity of the Academy this week. People are whispering about it.'

'I did notice that traffic seems to be detouring to avoid the Academy.'

'Word spreads. There are rumours of something dangerous within the Academy's walls—more dangerous than usual, I mean.' The Counsellor glanced at Meenakshi. 'Is there any way for you to know who cast any of the spells? Can you judge from the magical residues?'

'I can't. Chitralekha would know, but she saw everyone—*nearly* everyone—who might have caused the spike and she said it was none of them. She didn't see my father.'

'I think we can assume that the Governor is not responsible,' the Counsellor said dryly. 'For one thing, I doubt he would use the Academy basement to open a portal he could open with far greater convenience and far less possibility of detection in his own study ... But I suppose we shouldn't eliminate anyone until we're sure. You say it's simple magic to meddle with the statue?'

'Very simple,' said Kalban. 'As long as you were near enough to touch the statue. But the guards saw nobody suspicious in Temple Square.'

The Counsellor shrugged. 'I would more easily believe that the guards missed one person in a crowd hundreds strong than that someone managed a feat of magic from an impossible distance. Of everything that's happened, then, what requires the most difficult magic?'

Meenakshi exchanged a glance with Kalban.

'The portal,' they said together.

'Opening a portal is easy, but avoiding detection by the Border

Control Authority isn't,' Kalban explained. 'An Inter-Realm Portal can only be done from this side, which precludes the possibility of a rogue Sprite. And there aren't many people powerful enough to conceal even a normal portal from the sensors. One that moves? Very few would dare attempt it.'

'Who could have done it?'

Kalban counted off on his fingers. 'The Master Sorcerer. The Master of the Academy. Meenakshi, though I think she would have told me by now if it had been her doing.' Smiling at her exasperation, Kalban went on, 'The Chair of Summoning, the Chair of Alchemy. A couple of Dismissers from the Dangerous Beings Control Squad. Possibly the Chief of the Inter-Realm Liaison Bureau. I might just have been able to manage it, and so might a couple of other students.'

'I imagine the Chair of Summoning would have little need for portals ... and any of those people could open a portal with far more privacy in a secure location. It seems to me that the Academy basement suggests several people working together.'

'It would be unstable,' said Meenakshi. 'A portal needs focus.'

'I see your problem,' said the Counsellor. 'The individuals you mentioned are all monitored. If it had been any of them, the Inter-Realm Sensors would have picked up the spike. I'm no expert, but from what I've heard, those sensors could pick up a novice doing Levitation homework in the middle of Finals Week. That leaves one option. If it's not a *who*, then it must be a *what*.'

'You mean one of *them*?' Kalban asked. 'A djinn who crossed over and escaped his Summoner, or something?'

'It's likelier to be *or something*. We'd have to check the records at the border crossings. Unless ... I suppose an animal couldn't be causing this? The griffons, perhaps?'

'No,' Meenakshi said. 'We'd know. The sensors they have at the Arcane Zoology Authorisation Desk are just as strong as the ones in the Inter-Realm. I had eight of them show up at my door with indemnification forms as soon as I'd finished making the griffons. Besides ...' She shrugged. 'I felt the residues on the portal. No animal was responsible for that. Whatever it was, it was something at least as self-aware as a human.'

'Is it possible for someone to have made an animal that self-aware?'

'I doubt it,' said Kalban. 'People have tried, of course, but I've never heard of anyone being able to do it. You could create a body and give it life—that's just Alchemy—but you couldn't artificially create enough self-awareness that it could perform independent magic. Not such powerful magic.'

'In that case, we'll have to assume it's an illegal alien from the Inter-Realm,' said the Counsellor. 'You know what that means.'

Kalban sighed. 'I'll speak to the Chief of the Liaison Bureau.'

'And I'll tell you if I hear anything that might help your investigations.'

'You already know something that might help our investigations.' Meenakshi hadn't realised it until that moment but she knew it was true. It was easy to tell when the Counsellor was lying. He looked you in the eye with disconcerting earnestness when he did it. 'You're not telling us. Why not?'

He looked startled for a moment. Then he smiled. 'I gave up my bow many years ago, but nobody gives up the code of honour.'

Kalban looked as though he wanted to say something derogatory about the honour of Free Bows but didn't quite dare.

CHAPTER IX

'**Y**our father wants me to take my Tests,' Kalban said as he followed Meenakshi back into the corridor.

'Oh, good.'

Kalban stared at her. 'In which of the realms is that *good*?'

'In this one, I would have thought. You've been itching to get your licence for years.'

'Yes, but,' Kalban began. Then he trailed off. He couldn't begin to explain. He had spent a lot of time enumerating the advantages of having a licence, but that was only as a precaution against the possibility of Meenakshi deciding it was too much trouble to get one.

Besides, he thought, with more than a little frustration, it was a miracle that in the past two days his foster-sister had managed to speak to Avi, the professors at the Academy and the Counsellor without any casualties. It was too much to expect her to comprehend a situation as fraught as Kalban's would be once his father was free to demand his return.

'You wouldn't understand,' he said at last.

'Wouldn't I?'

Meenakshi studied him with the same unconcealed curiosity she had turned on Avi the previous afternoon. Kalban, being used to it, was less disconcerted, but he scowled all the same.

'It's rude to stare.'

'I remember you telling me that. You also told me it's unwise to lie to yourself. Do you think I don't know you're afraid to go home?'

'I am *not* afraid to go home!' Kalban snapped.

'Then maybe I'm wrong. What of it? You're afraid to go home, or you're not. What difference does it make to your Tests?'

Kalban thought he deserved some sort of special award for routinely dealing with this. He was the only person in the Free Lands who was required to do it. No human being but Meenakshi could be such a dismal failure at basic social interaction.

Fortunately, he was spared from having to formulate a response by the fact that they were now standing at the entrance to the Inter-Realm Liaison Bureau.

Kalban was, at any rate. Meenakshi was a good ten yards away.

'You'll handle this on your own, won't you?' she said. 'I don't like dealing with them.'

Kalban was about to protest. Meenakshi would one day succeed to her father's place as Governor, and she wouldn't have the advantage of a brother who could be sent to do things like *talk to people* while she sat poring over grimoires.

But he thought better of it. What she'd failed to learn in fourteen years she wouldn't learn in the next half hour. While he would have ignored her preferences in favour of her education, the fact was that the men and women in the Bureau didn't like dealing with her. At the moment, Kalban required their compliance, and Meenakshi's absence was the best means of procuring it.

In any case, he knew he wouldn't get Meenakshi into the Bureau without an argument. The middle of the corridor was hardly the place for it.

'Fine,' he said. 'Go back to the Palace and ... I don't know, study Philosophy. Or something that doesn't involve Chitralekha or Avi or any of *this*.'

Meenakshi looked startled, whether at his easy acquiescence or at the injunction to study Philosophy, Kalban didn't know. But she shrugged and nodded. Kalban decided that as long as she wasn't protesting, he didn't *have* to know.

'I'll study Philosophy, then.'

And Meenakshi was gone, leaving Kalban to knock on the large, ornately carved door.

The Inter-Realm Liaison Bureau involved a lot more due process, and a lot less getting to the point, than the Counsellor's realm. Kalban had the door opened to him by a woman who looked just a little *too* alive to be completely human. She led him to a waiting room and left him there with a form to fill out and instructions that not a single one of the thirty-four questions was to be omitted.

Kalban knew the room. The walls were covered in brocade and tapestries and the fittings were plated in solid gold set with glittering gems, rumoured to be gifts from the other Realm. It was impossible to say whether there was an echo of Chaos in their bright colours. The mingled heady scents of incense and sandalwood wafted from hidden brackets. Chords of sweet music, played from some concealed alcove, trembled and hung in the air before they dissipated.

It was where the Head of the Bureau, who was very alive to the befuddling effect of a concentrated assault on the senses, kept her visitors until she was ready for them—or judged them ready for her.

Kalban also knew the form. Its thirty-four questions were what the Head of the Bureau gave her visitors to keep them occupied while she decided what she wanted from them and how best to get it.

He flung the form aside and lowered himself onto the plump cushion the woman had indicated, but he didn't touch the spiced wine that just happened to be sitting on a small table within convenient reach. The Head of the Liaison Bureau was said to have had mutually beneficial liaisons with two successive Chairs of Alchemy at the Academy.

He'd been waiting for ten minutes, reciting the tenets of the Inter-Realm Code of Summoning under his breath, when the silk curtains at the far end of the room parted. Kalban stopped in the middle of the Rule of Seven Pentagrams to watch through narrowed eyes as a young man who was *definitely* half-Sprite shimmered into the room. He was beautiful in an inhuman way Kalban found terrifying.

'If you will follow me,' he said.

Kalban trailed after him down a narrow and winding—but be-tapestried—passage and up two flights of jewel-encrusted stairs before emerging onto a sunlit terrace.

Nalini, the Head of the Inter-Realm Liaison Bureau, was seated on a couch under a bright purple and gold awning. There was an empty chair beside her. At her nod, the young man offered it to Kalban.

'I'm delighted to see you.' Nalini's smile was brilliant and insincere. Kalban disliked her intensely, even if, unlike Meenakshi, he was capable of conducting a conversation with her like a civilised person. 'I wanted to speak to you. I was going to come by and see you tomorrow. Wine?'

'No, thank you,' Kalban said. It was best to leave no room for interpretation when speaking to Nalini.

'I tried talking to Asamanjas,' Nalini went on with a blithe laugh. 'Poor man. He's done so much for the city. I think he can afford to retire now, don't you? A nice villa in the countryside, some paddy fields, maybe a herd of cattle. I tried to tell him that. But the poor confused man just kept quoting the Prohibited and Conscripted Goods Act at me. I *know* Nectar is banned. I'm saying it *shouldn't* be.'

'It's a dangerous substance. It's highly addictive, it addles the brain, and, in large doses, it's lethal to mortals. It looks and smells like lemonade. Is this about the demigod who was trying to smuggle Nectar across the border?'

'You've heard about that? *Smuggle* is such a strong word ... Someone must have misrepresented the case to you. Poor bewildered Asamanjas, he should take a nice rest cure. He wasn't *smuggling*. He was travelling with a medicinal supply for his personal use. He *had* hoped to spend a week in Madh—I was going to ask him to address my young recruits on the subject of Inter-Realm relations in a new post-Accord era—but of course when the customs people confiscated all his Nectar, he had to go back almost at once.'

'He couldn't last a week without Nectar? I didn't realise demigods had less willpower than the average twelve-year-old.'

Nalini frowned. 'There's no need to be nasty about it.'

'He can get a letter from the Divine Physician, just like everyone else does. It's not like we don't know that claims of medical necessity are really admissions of low impulse control. And if you don't like the Prohibited and Conscripted Goods Act, you can submit a written amendment request to the Magical Activities Legislative Board. You know the procedure.'

'They questioned him for an entire *day*, Kalban.'

'That's a different issue. Did they attempt to bind him, restrain him or mistreat him in any way? Did they confiscate anything other than the contraband?'

'No, but—'

'In that case, if he has general complaints about how we handle contraband, they go in the suggestion box at the Customs Office. Forms are freely available.' Nalini glared at him. Kalban controlled his automatic reflex to glare back. He needed her tractable. 'All right. I'll look into it. I'm not promising anything. Nectar is prohibited for a reason. The Governor feels very strongly about it. But I'll see what I can do. Now can we please discuss what I came to talk about?'

'You didn't come here to discuss this egregious breach of Inter-Realm protocol?'

'I have reason to think there may be a rogue Sprite—or worse—loose in the city.'

'Impossible,' responded Nalini at once.

'Sprites and Celestial Dancers are the only beings permitted to materialise in the Mortal Realm un-Summoned at places other than the designated crossover points. If it's not one of them, it's something worse. If you help me, I might be able to sort this out without involving the Dangerous Beings Control Squad.'

Nalini shuddered. 'You wouldn't. There'll be an Inter-Realm incident! It took weeks of diplomacy and four state dinners to sort out the trouble after they arrested that djinn for Unauthorised Mortal Realm Spellcasting last year.'

'Help me, then.'

'What do you want?'

'I know you have sources of information on both sides of the border. I need to know who—or what—crossed over, and I need to know what they want.'

'I need time.'

'How much time?'

'Twenty-four hours. By then I'll either have an answer, or I'll know there isn't an answer I can give you.'

Kalban left, not ill-pleased to be finished with her. Spending any length of time with Nalini always left him wanting to attempt some ridiculous and dangerous alchemical spell. And Meenakshi and Paras did more than enough of that.

There was nothing more to be done that day. He could trust that one philosophical conundrum or another would keep Meenakshi occupied until she went to bed. He himself could retire to his room and think about something else.

His Tests, maybe.

Kalban groaned, but there was nothing for it. He had to write to his parents as well. He would do it as soon as he thought of a reasonable excuse to extend his absence from Melucha.

As soon as he stepped into the street, he was accosted by a blue-robed man who appeared to be about twenty feet tall. His form was obscured by his loose clothing, but it couldn't hide his muscular shoulders, over one of which he had slung a bow. There wasn't much of a crowd on the White Road that led from the Houses of Governance to the Palace and then on to the Academy, but such people as there were gave the man a wide berth.

'Not now,' Kalban told him. 'I heard about your friend, but I'm busy. File a complaint. I'll deal with it when I have time.'

'That's why I'm here,' the man said, in a voice that was intended to be menacing—that *would* have been menacing if they hadn't both known that Kalban could break his bow and melt his sword without stirring a step. 'We're not satisfied with the response we got to our last complaint. We got a stern note and a pamphlet about Section VII of the Magical Damage Act. Not even any recompense for emotional trauma!'

'Your last complaint was also about Meenakshi, wasn't it?'

'We're the Free Bows! Most people scream and beg when they see us! Nobody's prepared for ... nobody joins the Free Bows to be turned into a tortoise.'

'You're a bunch of idiots. You know what Section VII says! You are not entitled to reparations for trauma, injury or other damage caused by magic when you are deemed to have brought said trauma, injury or other damage on yourself by giving unreasonable provocation to a practitioner of magic. I think trying to sneak into her apartments is unreasonable provocation, don't you?'

'We weren't unreasonably provoking her! We were spying on her! That's what we *do*! The Act is biased towards practitioners. Why doesn't the Governor's daughter have to file a complaint instead of turning whoever she pleases into a tortoise?'

'Because your friend was trespassing on private property. If he'd tried to eavesdrop on Meenakshi in Temple Square, she would have had to file a complaint.'

'Chanura won't eat anything but grass and prickly pears!'

'She said she sent you a supply. The spell should wear off before it runs out.'

'You think this is about the cost of fruit? She's made it impossible for us to finish our assignment. Nobody's willing to go near the Palace. We'll have to refuse the job and return the deposit.'

'Declare the loss in your tax filing.'

'It's bad for business! A business like ours runs on reputation. Who's going to hire the Free Bows if we can't even carry out a basic spying operation on a teenage girl?'

'Maybe you'll all hang up your bows and become model citizens.'

'Maybe,' said another voice, as a grey-cloaked figure emerged from where it had been concealed by the great blue bulk of the Free Bow. 'Or maybe you'll see reason.'

Kalban concealed his surprise. The First Bow was no threat, not to him, but it was best to give him as little advantage as possible.

'Why would I do that?'

'Don't you want to know who hired us?'

'Do I care?'

'I think you will.'

Kalban crossed his arms. The Free Bows' honour was worth nothing, but they had sense enough to be cautious when dealing with people whose foster-sisters had been known to turn intruders into tortoises. They wouldn't offer him something they knew was worthless.

'What happened to client confidentiality?'

'We have a code,' the grey-robed man said. 'We don't tolerate threats to the order of the city.'

'Never mind your code. I'm sure you're not doing this at the dictates of your conscience. What do you want in exchange?'

'We want something to show our client.'

'I'm not going to give you permission to put a scorpion in Meenakshi's slippers.'

'We didn't think you would. Besides ... As I said, we don't tolerate threats to the order of the city. No matter what you think, that's true. Many of us have had our personal differences with your foster-sister, but I believe we all feel it is definitely in the better interests of Madh that she should live to take her father's place.'

'Fine. I'll talk to Meenakshi. You can enter the grounds, sidle around, stay clear of the Creeping Vine, and if you happen to find anything lying in the grass, you can take it to your client. If you manage to enter the public areas without getting caught, feel free to eavesdrop. If you or any weapon or projectile used by you gets within twenty feet of the Governor or his brother or daughter, you'll have to deal with the consequences. Private rooms are, as always, off limits if you want to leave the grounds in human form.'

'Fair enough. What about you, though?'

'You'll be getting within twenty feet of me,' Kalban said. 'I want to know every piece of information you pass on to your client.'

'Agreed.'

'Now tell me about your client.'

CHAPTER X

Meenakshi had Mathematics and Philosophy the next morning. Kalban didn't want to interfere with the schedule. That there were two tutors on the roster of the Royal Academy who could keep Meenakshi occupied for four hours between breakfast and lunch, and do so with none of the danger to life and property that came with a lesson in magic, was an extraordinary circumstance. It would take more than some practical paradoxes to make him disturb the arrangement. It would take more than an outright declaration of Inter-Realm war.

He didn't bother studying, although he had the morning free of lessons for that purpose. There were more important things to do.

The first important thing was to find out what people were saying about the God of Watchful Peace. The Accidental Magic Reversal Unit had sorted out the problem. It had taken ten minutes. Paras was unperturbed about the incident, Meenakshi had barely given it a second's thought, and even Asamanjas was sanguine.

Kalban couldn't help worrying.

In the tradition of generations of curious princes, he disguised himself before venturing into the street. Since this was Madh, the disguise consisted of a dark robe with a cowl pulled over his head, the sort of costume that would, in any other city, have marked him out as a threat to the peace and led to the appearance of a watchman with a stout stick. In Madh, the average citizen could expect to encounter at least four cowled figures on every trip to the vegetable market.

Normally nobody would have given Kalban a second glance, or even bothered to speak lower when he passed. Today, he spotted more than one sidelong stare. People didn't quite edge out of his path, but a surprising number of them found that the shortest route to their destination required crossing the street when they saw him coming.

That made it difficult to eavesdrop, but eventually Kalban discovered that, as he'd predicted, the general view seemed to be that it had been an amusing prank by one of the students. People in Madh were never short of excuses to point and gawk. Attention had already shifted to reports that one of the Cryptozoology fellows had fetched the phoenix from the Mountains of Ice and was attempting to breed it with a rain bird.

Kalban doubted that was true. The phoenix was notoriously bad-tempered, possibly the result of too much isolation. The rain bird didn't exist—or it hadn't until the previous week, when he'd received the monthly summary report of illicit activity from the Arcane Zoology Authorisation Desk.

But the idea seemed to amuse people. He wasn't about to argue with it, particularly when he saw that the strolling purveyors of protective amulets were doing brisk business.

That settled, he could move on to the second important thing—speaking to Avi's Professor of Applied Philosophy. Meenakshi hadn't given him more than a passing thought, though she'd sensed the residues of magic on him. That was typical of Meenakshi, but Kalban didn't intend to make the same mistake.

Avi's professor, who was also the Chair of Philosophy, was a forgettable man. Kalban himself had forgotten his name despite having been introduced to him on two separate occasions, and Kalban forgot names as frequently as he forgot to check his slippers for scorpions and his curtains for cobras. (Which, for anyone who had spent more than a week in the royal court of Melucha and had an aversion to death by venomous animal, was never.)

The Chair of Philosophy might have been as much of an idiot as both Paras and the Master of the Academy considered him. He lacked the power to have brought a Celestial Dancer across the border, since he was incapable of unleashing hellfire on an unsuspecting populace. But he had been in the presence of the source of the strangeness. A man who, despite his disadvantages, had managed to rise to the Chair of Philosophy, over several other candidates—and who had, if rumour was to be believed, been in the running for Master of the Academy, and might even have won if the Trustees hadn't deemed it necessary to have a practitioner of magic at the helm—might know something useful.

Kalban found the Professor of Applied Philosophy in his room in the Academy.

The Department of Philosophy occupied a single corridor—philosophers needed no laboratories, after all, nor magic-shielded practice rooms—tucked between the soundproof indoor amphitheatres of Rhetoric and the heavily guarded Summoning halls. The sounds of debate filtered through half-open doors. Kalban caught snatches of phrases like 'the personification of the deepest fear' and 'entertainment of ideas without acceptance'.

The office of the Chair of Philosophy was at the end of the corridor. Most heads of department decorated their doors with the symbols of their craft. Highly regarded scholars they might be, but they weren't above showing off. This door, though, was unadorned. It didn't even have the professor's name on it.

Kalban knocked.

'Come in!' a voice called.

The professor's voice was as unmemorable as he was. It was neither rough nor pleasing. His tone was just the right side of uninflected.

'Prince Heir,' the professor said.

Kalban started. It was the first time in months that anyone had addressed him by his formal title. Most people used his name, unless they were professors at the Academy, in which case they tended to address him as, 'You in the third row! I want you to rewrite your essay, and do it legibly this time!' Kalban would have liked to see them write in even lines if they had to deal with a good half of the administration of the city.

'I have questions,' he said, 'if you have a few moments.'

'Of course.'

'I believe you spoke to my sister yesterday.'

'I didn't think she'd remember.'

'She does.' Kalban hesitated. Embarrassing as it was for the Prince Heir of Melucha to admit, even to himself, now that he was in the midst of interrogating the professor, he had no idea how to phrase the question. He had to make it seem, while not an accusation of wrongdoing, nevertheless a question that must be answered truthfully, completely and immediately. He decided that he might as well just ask. 'Do you remember what you were doing just before you met her?'

'That's an unusual question.'

'Aren't unusual questions what the Academy is for?'

'That's what we put in the prospectus.' The professor shrugged. 'I don't remember. I suppose I must have been in class or at a staff meeting. We had the bi-monthly Inclusiveness Briefing yesterday. I went to it, but I don't know exactly what time I left. You can check the minutes.'

'Do you remember who else was at the briefing?'

'Why?' The professor smiled. 'Do you want to verify my story?'

'No.' Kalban paused again, thinking. What harm could it do? After all, there was no way the professor could be responsible for anything, except possibly the God of Watchful Peace. 'Meenakshi sensed the residues of magic on you. She thought you might have been in contact with somebody who ... who had been performing powerful spells.'

'That matters because of something to do with the Dancer from two days ago, I take it.' At Kalban's expression, the professor smiled. 'I'm not a sorcerer, Prince Heir, but I'm also not an idiot. Why don't you tell me what's been happening? Perhaps I can help.'

'It began with Avi,' Kalban started.

Twenty minutes later, he was winding up his story.

They sat in silence for a few moments after that, while the professor fiddled with a stack of essays on his desk.

'I don't know that I can help you,' he said at last. 'I wasn't with anyone who could have done what you describe. The Master of the Academy never attends Inclusiveness Briefings. He considers them a waste of time. Other than that, most of my day was spent with my students—your friend Avi among them. If you want to speak to them ...' He made a negligent gesture.

Kalban felt out of his depth. He was adept at knowing what people wanted and using it to make them reasonable. He could successfully read human beings, Sprites, djinn, nagas and Meenakshi, and he was certain he was the only person in the city who could say that.

He had a strong feeling that the professor was lying, but he couldn't say how or why. It made him feel ridiculous, and he hated feeling ridiculous.

This had been the most appalling waste of time.

'Thank you.' He got to his feet.

'Goodbye.'

Kalban left, shutting the door behind him, and found himself face-to-face with Avi.

'What are you doing here?' his friend demanded. 'You don't take a single Philosophy course.'

'I wanted to speak to your professor.'

'Why?'

'Does it matter?' Kalban asked, a little startled by Avi's vehemence. 'I thought he might know something.'

'You told him—' Avi's hand shot out and caught and Kalban's sleeve. 'What did you tell him? What did you say?'

'Only what you told me. What's wrong?'

'*You told him everything*?' Avi sounded angry, which was a surprise. He had never before displayed any violent emotion other than terror. '*Why?* Why would you do that?'

The only thing Kalban could think of to say was 'Why not?' That was the kind of half-witted thing Meenakshi tended to say, so he decided it was best to let Avi go on uninterrupted.

'I would have told him myself, if I'd wanted him to know!'

'You didn't object to my telling Meenakshi!' Kalban protested. 'How was I to imagine you'd object to my telling anybody else?'

'Why would I object to your telling Meenakshi?'

'Because most people object to telling Meenakshi anything. She's got no sense of discretion.'

'It looks like she's not the only one!' Avi shook his head. 'I'm sorry. I suppose it's my fault for not telling you to keep it quiet. It's just—there's no sense talking to—I was—I must have been imagining things. We can just forget about it. I'm sure there's nothing.'

'We can't forget about it.'

'I told you! I must have imagined the noises!'

'Maybe you did. I'd say for once in your life you didn't imagine noises, but we can let that slide. Even if you did imagine the noises, nobody imagined the Inter-Realm Sensors going off ... or the God of Watchful Peace deciding to become the God of Gently Smiling Meditation. Did you hear about that?'

'This is Madh! Strange things are always happening. That's the chief attraction of the city. It's in the tourist brochure!'

Kalban studied his friend. 'What are you afraid of?'

'I'm not afraid of anything.' Avi crossed his arms. 'If you must know, I have Tests coming up in a couple of months.'

Kalban hadn't known that, but he wasn't surprised. The month after Finals Week was normally devoted to the Tests for the Magic Licence. Without a master to interfere with the timing, Avi was free to take his Tests whenever he wanted. He'd taken them every year since his fifteenth birthday—this would be his third attempt.

'That doesn't explain why you don't want your professor to know about your noises. Last year, you spent the week before your Tests telling us all about how a rogue Sprite in the amphitheatre made you fail your Rhetoric final.'

'That was last year. I *have* to pass this year, Kalban. I need my licence. I *can't* stay here longer. And if he thinks I've been imagining things—or spreading rumours—he won't give me a passing grade in Uncommon Sense.'

'He gave you a passing grade last year, and you told him about the rogue Sprite too.'

'This is different! Let this go, Kalban!' The hall gong rang its sonorous note, marking the hour. Avi gave a start. 'I have Ethics of Alchemy. I have to go. Please, just … forget I said anything.'

He ran away, leaving Kalban staring after him.

Kalban followed more slowly. He would have given a great deal to know why Avi wanted him to give up so badly. He would have given even more to know the professor's mind. Avi clearly didn't intend to be helpful. That meant they would have to rely on other means to find out where the professor had been.

Scrying was a possibility. Maybe. Bending time in a scrying bowl had to be much harder than bending space. It would be a violation of the Code of Ethics. In any case, the Master of the

Academy claimed it couldn't be done. So did Paras. Kalban was certain that Paras, at least, had attempted it.

If there was a way to prove the matter once and for all, it was to go to Meenakshi and tell her that scrying into the past was impossible.

Kalban shook himself, appalled that he'd even considered it.

Just as he emerged into the main hall, light flashed as the silent alarm went off.

CHAPTER XI

Kalban hadn't been wrong to think that Meenakshi's Mathematics and Philosophy lessons would keep her occupied through most of the morning. Where he had erred had been in disregarding the good use to which she could put the hours between dinner and the time her tutors arrived to claim her attention after breakfast, and the chain of events she could set in motion in that period.

Meenakshi had woken suddenly in the middle of the night. This, in itself, was no cause for concern. But while most people would have rolled over and gone back to sleep, or sought the assistance of a glass of warm milk, Meenakshi sat up in bed and lit a lamp with a snap of her fingers.

Experience had taught her to be quiet. She was alone in her bedroom, but the rooms to either side of hers each housed a lynx-eared secretary. She had often argued against the arrangement, which was a tradition that was both archaic and anachronistic. Kalban agreed that it was archaic, conceded that Meenakshi was capable of defending herself against any midnight marauders who weren't caught by the Creeping Vine, and then went on to explain that he wasn't as worried about who might sneak in as he was about what Meenakshi might bring in. Griffons, for example, or cobras, and did Meenakshi recall the incident with the Sprite, the figs and the fourteen cats?

The Governor's Palace in Madh, unlike many other fortresses and palaces in the kingdom, had no secret passages. Meenakshi wouldn't have bothered with them if there had been any. Secret passages were dank and unpleasant and you came out smelling like moss and stale air, which was a dead giveaway that you'd been in one.

Meenakshi took the lamp and left her room by the door.

A simple Illusion meant the guards never saw her walk out. She couldn't do anything to keep them from hearing her. But her slippers didn't make much noise on the polished granite floors. In any case, the guards inside the Governor's Palace were as inured to unexplained noises as the citizens outside it were to mysterious cloaked figures.

Meenakshi hadn't planned on any midnight wandering when she'd gone to bed. But, having woken up, it had occurred to her that an Inter-Realm portal couldn't stay open on its own indefinitely, and that whoever had opened the one in the Academy basement would either have to renew it or let it close.

Meenakshi didn't normally care about chasing down wrongdoers as much as some people, such as her uncle and her foster-brother. But her curiosity had been piqued by the portal. She hadn't known it was possible, she hadn't considered attempting such a thing herself—and although she agreed with Kalban that unauthorised portals were dangerous, she very much wanted to know how it had been achieved.

There were no secret passages in the Governor's Palace, or for that matter, anywhere in the city of Madh, but there was a vast and un-secret underground network of tunnels connecting basements and cellars around the city. The tunnels tended to be empty of people, because students at the Academy frequently used them to practice curse-setting. This was encouraged by the Master of the Academy and the Captain of the City Guard, particularly in the areas surrounding the vaults under the Governor's Palace and the Academy basements.

As a result, no part of the underground was truly safe. Not even the Free Bows would want to run afoul of a teenage apprentice's first attempt at a booby-trap when they could sneak into their targets' homes through perilously high windows, risking no more than a broken leg.

Normally, Meenakshi wouldn't have taken the tunnels. Although, like most students, she knew what and where most of the spells were, the novelty of running their gauntlet had worn off after the first few times. But, at the moment, the tunnels provided her the best means of getting to the Academy undetected: the guards at the Palace gates weren't nearly as easy to fool as the ones outside her apartments.

She slipped through them in near-total darkness, the flickering light from her lamp making odd shadows in front of her. The necessity of disabling or evading traps meant it was a longer walk than it would have been by the road.

As she neared the room where the portal had been, she heard voices, and drew to a halt.

She stayed out of sight, peering around the edge of the doorway. The portal was there, but this time there was light shining through it, so bright that everything else in the room was cast into murky shadow. Meenakshi thought she could see movement, but she couldn't tell who, or how many people. Her senses were tingling in the way that usually indicated the presence of a being from the Inter-Realm, but she couldn't be sure it wasn't just the portal.

Meenakshi straightened and considered her options. She didn't enjoy cloak-and-dagger operations, but she *did* want to know how the portal was being held.

'You shouldn't be here.'

Meenakshi whirled, opening her mouth angrily at the sight of the slender figure that had appeared behind her. Chitralekha smiled, but her eyes were grave.

'Don't argue. I know you can sense it.' She waved her hand in the direction of the room. 'That thing is dangerous to mortals. Whoever's doing it ...'

'What are you doing here? Weren't you supposed to stay away until tomorrow?'

'I did what I said. I tried to find the portal from the other side, and when *that* started happening to it, I managed to slip through without anybody noticing.'

'You're here illegally?'

'Is this the time to lecture me about standing in line at the border crossing turnstiles and filling in the form?'

'I don't care about the form. But Kalban will.'

'Kalban doesn't have to know—until tomorrow, when you'll Summon me and I'll be here legally.'

'That's the spike, isn't it?' Meenakshi asked, looking into the room again. The light seemed even brighter now. 'The spike on the Inter-Realm Sensors.'

'It must be. But who is it?'

'*What* is it? Something must have come through the portal.'

'I can't tell,' Chitralekha murmured.

'I could scry—'

'Too dangerous. We don't know what's causing the spike. It might be something that can trace backwards to you.'

All of a sudden, the light faded. Meenakshi quickly pressed herself against the wall, out of sight of the people in the room. Chitralekha backed away next to her.

'There *is* something,' Chitralekha said. 'Something from the Inter-Realm, but not a very powerful something.'

Meenakshi stared at her. 'It *must* be powerful. A Level V demigod passing through the portal wouldn't cause that spike.'

'No, listen to me.' Chitralekha tugged her further away from the door. 'If there's some Inter-Realm being or creature powerful enough to cause the kind of spikes the sensors have been picking up, and that we just saw, it should cause an equivalent dip when it crosses back. But we haven't had a single significant dip in months.'

'You mean the spikes were caused by things crossing over ... And they're still here?' Meenakshi shook her head. 'No. We'd know.'

'Hasn't this been the week for impossible things?'

'Yes, but not that kind of impossible. Nobody's been able to produce a moving portal yet, but it's possible someone might have worked it out. Someone might have smuggled Nectar through the customs posts. The border guards are as prone to error as anyone. Someone, or maybe several someones, might have caused that first spike you saw with a spell whose effects aren't outwardly visible. But it *isn't* possible that an independent source of magic that strong could cross over and stay here without being detected.'

Chitralekha worried her lip. 'You're right. We'd still see increased output, and you'd sense the residues wherever it went. Unless someone created an antimagic field—'

'An antimagic field powerful enough to contain that level of output? It would throw out all natural law. Gravity, magnetism, nothing would work—'

'It could be controlled.'

'Someone would have to be strong enough—' Meenakshi's eyes narrowed. 'I didn't do it.'

'I'm not saying you did!'

Chitralekha's voice rose a little on the last word. All conversation inside the room ceased at once. Rapid footsteps advanced in their direction.

'Go!' Meenakshi said, taking another step away from the doorway.

'But you—'

'They'll never find me in these passages. If they have any sense, they won't even try. Go. I'll see you tomorrow—but don't come until I Summon you, or Kalban won't sleep for a week.' The footsteps were almost upon them. *'Go.'*

Chitralekha vanished.

Meenakshi briefly considered laying a couple of spells to aid her departure. But spells might be traced to her, and she didn't want anyone complaining to Kalban before she got a chance to tell him herself. Instead of returning the way she had come, she slipped into a tunnel whose entrance was half-hidden behind a sculpture of the Great Sorceress Anasuya. It was narrow and twisting and, indeed, it smelled of damp and moss, making it in every respect the sort of tunnel Meenakshi deplored.

But it had the advantage of allowing the passage of only one person at a time.

Meenakshi couldn't help a small, amused smile to herself as she heard the echoes of several pairs of feet, and muffled curses as the owners of the feet bumped into each other. Infuriating though it was when her foster-brother insisted on quoting passages from *Cloak and Dagger: A Guide to Navigating the Princely Court of Melucha,* she would have to stop complaining quite so much. And maybe even read the book herself.

She paused to conjure a thick mist behind her. It was a basic spell, unlikely to be identifiable as her handiwork, and it wouldn't hold her pursuers for long. But it would give her a few moments.

She came to a fork in the tunnel—a triple fork to those who knew just where to press the wall to open the hidden door, and a double fork to anyone who had never been a student at the Academy. She had bought herself enough time to take a second to consider. *Cloak and Dagger* would tell her to open the hidden door, pass through it, and climb the small flight of stairs on the other side. It would take her to street level, to the ever-bustling streets of Madh, and the authors of *Cloak and Dagger* placed great reliance on the safety of crowds.

That was where Meenakshi had a difference of opinion with the authors of *Cloak and Dagger*.

She opened the door, closed it again, and took the right fork. After a minute or so, it broadened and gave onto the vaults below the Governor's Palace.

She stood behind a convenient pillar, and watched.

She heard people approach the fork, and heard their rapid conversation as they decided to split into pairs to follow all three paths. *Cloak and Dagger* would approve. Four pairs of footsteps died away, and two approached her admittedly not clever hiding place. Meenakshi wasn't worried. Unless one of those two turned out to be the Master of the Academy or the Chair of Summoning, she could take care of herself.

When they emerged into the relative brightness where the tunnel widened, Meenakshi suppressed a gasp.

One of those people was *Avi*. He was carrying a torch, and she could recognise him by its light.

The other was a man she barely noticed. Her eyes slid over him to Avi, and then sharply back when she remembered that Kalban would expect a description, and would lecture her for hours if she failed to provide one that satisfied him.

The man was wrapped in a cloak so black it seemed to suck in all light. He was tall and, as far as she could judge, slender, but she could see nothing of his face, concealed by a fold of his cloak. She was as accustomed to mysterious cloaked figures as any citizen of Madh, but this man was not mysterious. He was ...

He was one of *them*.

Her senses tingled as he approached and she knew she was right.

She thought she knew *what* he was, too. Kalban had once told her of an old Meluchan legend of Hidden Men—the same creatures that could eat magical residues, now that she thought of it.

But—no. He'd said it was no more than a legend. There was no record of Hidden Men, not even in the books of the Inter-Realm Liaison Bureau. It was—

Just as they were about to find her, there was a high, unearthly shriek, and the nerve-destroying screech of sharp claws on wet stone. A shadow descended from the ceiling above them. It was illuminated for a moment by the torch, broad, powerful wings, and the glimmer of a predator's eyes.

Avi screamed.

Then he turned and fled.

Meenakshi didn't see his companion run, but he must have done, because, between one moment and the next, he was gone.

She let out a breath and turned to the creature that had now landed and was carefully folding its massive wings. It looked as awkward on the ground as it had looked deadly in the air. When Meenakshi patted its head, it made a contented sound that was half-squawk and half-purr, and rolled onto its back, waving its forelegs—an eagle's talons—and its hind legs—a lion's paws—in the air.

Meenakshi had heard plenty of debates on the morality of creating living creatures through Alchemy. The head of the Arcane Zoology Authorisation Desk had made a point of sending her several articles and a detailed treatise on the subject. She herself had never been conflicted about the ethics of what she occasionally did. People bred horses. People bred cattle. The court bards said that people in Vraja bred crocodiles. Why shouldn't Meenakshi breed griffons?

And Alchemy was a far more precise science than animal husbandry. There were rules. What came out of the Alchemical Incubator could never be more or less than what went in, and if you wanted to create a powerful predator, you needed powerful ingredients. Yaunic historians described huge, fierce, winged eagle-headed lions that tore intruders to shreds. It was possible to make animals that were fierce, if you were willing to milk tigresses and tickle scorpions to extract their venom.

Willing, perhaps, was the wrong word. Alchemists had been willing, in the past, but tigresses and scorpions had been unwilling. Meenakshi's sympathy was with the animals. If you tried to milk a tigress that didn't want to be milked, you deserved to come home covered in claw marks.

As for size, not even Alchemy was stronger than Aerodynamics.

With normal agents, what you'd find in the Academy's Alchemy lab or any respectable Alchemical supplies store, all you could make was what Meenakshi had done—griffons with twelve-foot wingspans and bodies the size of half-grown wolves, cheerful animals that screeched happily at intruders and rolled over to have their bellies rubbed if anyone came near them. You couldn't make anything dangerous.

Of course, burglars lacked both knowledge of advanced Alchemical theory and the ability to distinguish happy shrieks from murderous shrieks, which was why the griffons had proved a useful deterrent in the vaults.

'And how did *you* get here?' Meenakshi asked the griffon. It made no answer other than a squawk. She considered it for a moment and then shrugged. 'I suppose you'd better come with me, then.'

With the griffon trailing behind her in its odd lopsided gait, its mismatched feet shuffling and clicking and oversized wings trailing on the floor, she made her way back to her room.

CHAPTER XII

ost people, having discovered that their foster-brother's friend had been telling blatant lies, as well as consorting with a terrifying creature hitherto believed only legend, would have spent a sleepless night, and would, in all likelihood, have ensured that that foster-brother spent a sleepless night as well.

Meenakshi was not most people.

She returned to the Palace, using a simple Illusion to conceal the griffon from the guards. She settled the griffon down in a corner of her room on a cushion, where it would be found by her secretaries the next morning. (Fortunately, Meenakshi's secretaries were both strongly constituted, accustomed to sudden shocks and fond of animals.)

The next morning, as Kalban had intended, Philosophy and Mathematics took Meenakshi's attention, and it was some time before she recollected that she had been out of bed the previous night.

As soon as she remembered, she went back for the griffon. She found it sunning itself by the window in her study, beak-deep in what had once been a bowl of fruit but was now a mess of juice, pips and bits of pulp.

'It didn't want to eat anything less ... moist?' Meenakshi asked Saha, who was watching it.

'We tried the strips of dried meat the falconer uses. It turned up its beak at that. Apparently, it's still a herbivore.'

'I did think that might happen when I used cows' milk. We should try the feed mix they use in the stables. That might be neater.'

'I could find out what they feed the griffons in the vaults, if you're planning on keeping this one.'

'We'll have to see about that.' Meenakshi bent to scratch the griffon's head. 'You can be sure Kalban will have something to say on the subject.' She snapped her fingers in front of the griffon's face. 'Come. If we're going to persuade Kalban and Uncle Asamanjas to let you stay in the Palace, you're going to have to prove your usefulness.'

She didn't go back underground. After the previous night, she no longer had the advantage of surprise. She put a cloaking spell on the griffon and took it through the streets to the Academy. If she hadn't been distracted by thoughts of Avi, the Hidden Man, and what Kalban would have to say about everything, she would have been delighted to see how well the Illusion worked. The difficulty of the spell increased with the number of people who had to be misled, and Meenakshi had never before cast one strong enough to keep the throng loitering on the streets of Madh from seeing a live griffon walking through their midst.

Meenakshi got the griffon inside the Academy grounds and to the top of the basement steps, fortunately encountering none of the professors on the way. She didn't have time to revel in her good fortune, though, because barely had she laid a hand on the door than there was a spark of *something* and the silent alarm went off.

Meenakshi scowled. She should have considered that possibility. She was slipping.

She caught the griffon by the scruff of the neck, thanking her lucky stars that it was good-tempered, and hauled it away in the direction of the river gate. Nobody would take that way out; evacuation protocol meant everyone would use the main exit to the courtyard. The griffon's talons clattered on the stone floor. Meenakshi cursed. Now that the alarm had been sounded, she couldn't do any spellcasting within the perimeter walls.

'Fly,' she hissed at it, tugging its head upward for added emphasis. 'That'll be quieter.'

Whether it understood her words or the gesture she didn't know; at any rate, with a couple of beats of its powerful wings, it was in the air.

'Now *come*.'

She doubled around the back of the building. As soon as she was within sight of the courtyard, she urged the griffon into a large jasmine bush. 'Stay,' she hissed, straightening and looking around.

On the far side of the courtyard, at the main entrance to the building, the Master of the Academy and half a dozen members of the Dangerous Beings Control Squad were speaking to—

Avi.

Meenakshi stiffened. Avi probably hadn't seen her the previous night, and there was no way he could know what had happened just now. And in any case, she hadn't done anything wrong. Contrary to the spirit of the pamphlets the Arcane Zoology Authorisation Desk was always leaving outside her door, yes, but not *wrong*.

All the same, Kalban and her uncle wouldn't leave off lecturing her for weeks.

Then, to make matters worse, Kalban himself emerged from the building and went over to the group. He exchanged a few words with them, looked around, and saw Meenakshi. He looked more resigned than unhappy as he made his way across the courtyard to her. Maybe she would escape the lecture.

'Did you sense anything?' Kalban asked as soon as he was within earshot.

That had been the last question Meenakshi had expected, so he had to repeat it twice before she remembered to answer.

'What did Avi say?' she demanded.

'He said he set off the alarm.'

Meenakshi stared. If Avi had set off the alarm, had it been mere coincidence that she had laid a hand on the door at the same time? But—no. She had seen the spark. And the first lesson in Kalban's forsaken books on Political Science was that nothing was ever a coincidence.

'He pulled an emergency lever. He heard something,' Kalban went on, for once so absorbed in his thoughts that he hadn't noticed Meenakshi's reaction. 'Or maybe sensed something, or ... you know the rest of it, I'm sure. Were you inside the building?'

'Yes.' The jasmine bush began to quiver, and Meenakshi stuck her hand in it to soothe the griffon. 'I didn't sense anything, though.' She drew a deep breath. 'And Avi didn't set off the alarm.'

Kalban's brows drew together. 'How do you know?'

'Because I did—oh, don't look so disapproving. I didn't intend to!'

'You don't even *have* an Alchemy lab scheduled this week, so you couldn't have had an accident. What happened?'

'It's a long story. I'll tell you later. Don't you have to deal with your crazy friend?'

'Avi isn't crazy.'

Meenakshi didn't know why he bothered; it wasn't like he was fooling anyone. And it wasn't like Meenakshi cared. Some people were sane, some people weren't. She didn't judge.

'Isn't he?' she asked. 'He just took responsibility for an alarm he didn't set off. And look at him.'

Kalban turned to where Avi was saying something urgent, if the vehemence of his gesticulation was any indication, to the Master of the Academy. Meenakshi took the opportunity to pat the griffon's head and withdraw her hand from the bush.

'He's frightened,' Kalban said dismissively.

'There's no reason to be frightened. It's an alarm. They happen all the time … Well, I suppose Avi has a reason to be frightened.'

Kalban spun to face her. 'What do you know?'

'This isn't the time or the place. We can discuss it later.'

'Meenakshi, don't be more of a fool than you must. Whatever we're dealing with, it's powerful. You can't take it on by yourself. Not even you.'

'Don't be ridiculous,' Meenakshi said shortly. 'I'm not taking anything on. Go. Deal with your friend. Give him tea or milk or spiced wine, or whatever it is people in Melucha drink when they need to calm down. I'll discuss this with you at home.'

'Are you going home now?'

'I ... I think I'll stay here, just for a bit. Just to ... soak in the atmosphere.'

Kalban stopped short in the act of stepping away, and Meenakshi knew she'd been caught. She should have thought of a better excuse. Nobody who knew her would believe that she would choose to remain in a crowd of students when she could be elsewhere.

On cue, the bush quivered.

Kalban's eyes narrowed.

'You brought something,' he accused in a low hiss.

'Shhhh! I didn't bring him—well, I did, but, really, he came and found me. I thought he'd be useful. They have a natural ability to find secret rooms. But the alarm went off and I had to bring him out.'

'Him?'

'The griffon. It's a long story. I'll explain later.'

'You brought a *griffon* to the Academy?'

'I'll explain later.'

'Is that what set off the alarm?'

'Of course not. I had him cloaked.'

Kalban's expression turned into worry. 'Meenakshi—'

'He was fine! It was when I touched the basement door—'

'You were going into the *basement*? Forget Avi, you're the one who's insane. We have no idea what might be down there.' Then he frowned, watching her carefully. 'We have no idea what might be down there, do we, Meenakshi?'

'I said I would discuss it with you *later*.'

Kalban looked like he was going to argue, but in the end he gave in. 'All right. Wait here until everyone's inside and then take the griffon back. Go home and *stay* there until I come. Please, just this once, don't do anything stupid.'

As Kalban walked away, Meenakshi dropped to a crouch and slipped her hand into the foliage again. A feathered head was thrust against her fingers.

'That's right,' Meenakshi whispered. '*Such* a good boy. Stay quiet, now, and we'll slip away when all these dreadful people have gone.'

'Meenakshi?'

Meenakshi straightened and faced the speaker, a girl about her own age. Her face was vaguely familiar. Meenakshi had a faint memory of having been introduced to her and forced to endure two hours of small talk, and a stronger memory of discussing potential causes for the last alarm with her a couple of days ago. But for the life of her she couldn't remember the girl's name.

A few months ago, Meenakshi would have made abortive, painfully obvious attempts to remember her name and let herself in for a lecture from Kalban. Now, with the advantage of experience, she smiled brightly and said, 'How nice to see you again!'

'Did you have a class? I thought you said you didn't take classes at the Academy.'

'Um,' said Meenakshi, who, as recent events had shown, was never much good at thinking up believable stories under pressure. 'Do you know what this to-do is all about?'

The girl tossed her head. 'They're saying it was Avi sounding the alarm. It could be anything. Maybe he saw his own shadow.

He's always been jumpy, and he's been worse ever since he quit the Applied Philosophy Club.'

'Avi quit the Applied Philosophy Club?'

'Weird, isn't it? Considering how pally he is with their faculty advisor and all the other members. And *nobody* quits the Applied Philosophy Club. It's like one of those cults where the only way to leave once they've got their claws in you is to be strangled with your own scarf and dumped in an alley.' Meenakshi's expression must have reflected alarm, because the girl went on, 'Oh, I don't mean they kill people or anything. They're just—you know—*nasty* to people who leave. They've got a high opinion of themselves. They think they're more useful than philosophers and more intellectual than practitioners of magic.'

'That's ...' Meenakshi tried to find a suitable comment, 'odd ...'

The girl nodded emphatically. '*Odd* just describes it. And they're getting odder. They're all so jumpy lately. Jumping at shadows, jumping at noises. You should have heard Gargi shriek in the Alchemy lab last week just because her draught hissed a little. And did you hear they nearly came to blows with the Numerology Club? None of them can cast spells worth anything —well, Manu can, and so can Gargi when she's not trying to hide from a sputtering potion. And I suppose Jai's all right.'

'So they ... had a fight with the Numerology Club?'

'They were lucky their professor put a stop to it before anyone got hurt. They all had to write essays about the proper comportment for magicians-in-training who hope not to be magicians-in-training forever.'

'*Avi* came to blows with the Numerology Club?' Meenakshi asked incredulously. She couldn't imagine Avi coming to blows with anyone. She could, however, imagine him seeing other people coming to blows with each other and proceeding with all possible haste in the opposite direction.

'Of course not *Avi*,' the girl said with open scorn. 'Catch *him*. Raman's in Numerology and Avi is terrified of him.'

'Clever Raman?'

'Yes, how many Ramans are there? Do you know him?'

'Not in particular,' Meenakshi said, adding firmly, 'and I do *not* want to be introduced to him.'

'Really? I'd've thought he'd be just your type. He's strange too.' The girl looked suddenly horrified. 'That is—not that I think you're strange or—I don't—um—that's not important. Anyway, I heard it all. I was there. Raman accused Manu—he's the head of the Applied Philosophy Club, see him over there?'

'The one explaining the concept of Self to a squirrel?'

'No, that's Manu's friend Jai. Jai's the founder-president of the Fourth Debate Society. And also its only member.'

'There are four debating societies?' asked Meenakshi, fascinated. She would have to come to the Academy more often.

'Oh, no, there's one, and it's called the Debating Society. Last year's competitions were hotly contested and the Fourth Debate—that's the last debate on Debate Day, the grand finale— was between Jai and Kashyap. Kashyap won, but Jai maintains that the judges were biased because Kashyap's parents are in the diamond mining business. He formed the Fourth Debate Society to arrive at the truth.'

'What was the Fourth Debate about?'

'The ethics of creating living creatures through Alchemy. Frankly, I've always found that a little creepy. How do you feel about it?'

'Oh, look,' said Meenakshi. 'They're letting people back in.'

'Thank the *gods*!' exclaimed the girl. 'I had elixir brewing in the Alchemy lab!'

And she was off like a bolt from a crossbow.

All around, students were reluctantly abandoning the courtyard to return to their classrooms and workshops. Meenakshi didn't move. As docile as the griffon was, she didn't want to risk it getting caught.

Meenakshi couldn't move, but she could think, and she applied herself to the task. Her tutors in Mathematics, Alchemy, Summoning, History and Philosophy hadn't been exaggerating when they described her as brilliant. Nature, perhaps appreciating the handicap she would suffer all her life in her inability to participate in the small deceptions that are a part of modern society, had compensated her with a mind capable of flying where other minds walked.

Her mind was flying now, swift and sure, and the nameless girl had shown her the way.

She had told the Counsellor that the sensors at the Arcane Zoology Authorisation Desk were strong, and that had been the truth. She herself had never been able to fool them. It was unlikely anyone else had managed it.

But the sensors at the Arcane Zoology Authorisation Desk only detected Alchemy.

The girl, whose name Meenakshi really ought to find out, had mentioned a debate on the ethics of creating living creatures through Alchemy. But the rules of Alchemy were precise. What went in was what came out. Alchemy couldn't cause unexplained spikes on the Inter-Realm Sensors.

Absently, Meenakshi thrust her hand into the bush to pet the griffon again.

Alchemy was a precise science, but Applied Philosophy was ...

Meenakshi didn't know. Nobody quite understood Applied Philosophy, the Applied Philosophers least of all.

It was harmless, though. At least, the Applied Philosophy they taught at the Academy was harmless. There were no practical exercises, just discussions of possibilities. There couldn't be practical exercises; Applied Philosophy was too little understood and far too dangerous.

Meenakshi had an idea—if a vague, unformed idea—why that was.

Alchemy converted matter to other matter, and sometimes converted back and forth between matter and energy. It was logical. There were rules, as inviolable as the rules of the physical sciences. If you wanted a fierce monster, you had to milk a tigress. Or find someone in a shady back-alley Alchemical supplies shop to do it for you. *Someone* had to milk a tigress. If you milked a cow ...

Meenakshi patted the griffon's head. The bush quivered as it wriggled in glee.

This was what you got if you milked a cow.

Applied Philosophy was limited only by the imagination of its adherents. In Meenakshi's admittedly limited experience, the politer practitioners of magic were, the darker the landscapes of their thoughts.

Thoughts festered. And it was dangerous for a magician's thoughts to fester.

Meenakshi felt a chill creep up her spine.

CHAPTER XIII

'Are you sure?' Kalban asked. Even as he formed the words, he knew it was a stupid question. There was only one way to be sure.

'Of course I'm not sure!' Meenakshi snapped, her face creasing into a scowl right on cue. 'I was going to make sure as soon as the commotion died down and everyone was back in class but *somebody* dragged me off before I could go in and check.'

'You can't just walk into things without a plan! If your theory is right, you might have ended up confronting—I don't even know what you might have ended up confronting! This is beyond the rules of Alchemy. Anything might happen.'

'Not *anything*,' said Meenakshi. '*Anything* can never happen, not even in the Inter-Realm. This thing might not obey the rules of Alchemy, but it has to obey *some* rules.'

'It has a form,' ventured Chitralekha, whom Meenakshi had finally Summoned. 'Or it seemed to. If it's taken a physical form in the Mortal Realm, there are limits to its power. If we can find out what they are, we'll know what to do.'

'You,' Kalban growled, turning on her. '*You*, I will deal with later. What were you thinking last night, encouraging her to loiter in the basement spying on miscreants? She could've been killed!'

Meenakshi glared at him. 'Your crazy friend seemed to be able to handle it just fine.'

'This isn't the kind of magic you're used to. Maybe it follows rules, but we have no idea what they are. You would have been going in blind against something far more dangerous than you can imagine.' Meenakshi rolled her eyes. 'I'm not being melodramatic,' Kalban went on. 'Think about just how powerful an unrestricted mind can be.'

'Powerful,' Meenakshi said, 'but not harmful. Thoughts never hurt anyone.'

'That's the point, though, isn't it? Thoughts don't always stay thoughts. They turn into more.' He turned to Chitralekha. 'Did you find out anything about it? Could she be right? Could someone have *willed* this creature into existence?'

'It's possible. I can't give you a more definite answer than that. How much do you know about how an immortal species comes to be?'

'Nothing,' said Kalban. 'Nobody knows. I always thought it was a closely-guarded secret.'

'It's not a secret at all. There was a time, long ago, when mortals knew. I suppose the storytellers of the age thought it was so self-evident a truth that it didn't need to be written.' Chitralekha shrugged. 'In time, the story faded from mortal knowledge. Philosophers started debating the matter. None of them thought of asking the ones likeliest to know the truth ... and we didn't volunteer the information.'

'Tell us, then,' said Meenakshi. 'How does an immortal species come to be?'

'It happens when mortals believe in something intensely enough. It sounds simple when I put it like that, but it's not. Pretending to believe isn't enough. Wanting to believe isn't enough. Rambha was the earliest of the Dancers—one of the earliest of any of the immortal beings—and she's told me what the world of mortals was then.'

'What was it?' Kalban asked.

'It was dark. You were still evolving from apes—and I mean that in the most complimentary possible way. Mortals were *evolving*. Their minds were awakening to independent thought. Before that, they'd only known what animals knew— hunger and thirst, the need for warmth and the need for safety. But there came a time when their baser needs were satisfied. That was when they learnt to want *more*, to want answers. They wanted to know why the sun rose and why the cold wind blew from the north. They wanted to know who sent the rain and who lit the stars. They guessed at these things, and they believed their own guesses. They *needed* to believe their own guesses, because they needed to *know*, and they refused to believe that knowledge was impossible.'

'And they believed intensely enough to make the *gods*?' Kalban said in disbelief.

'No, not exactly. They didn't *make* the gods; after all, there was already a sun and there was already rain and the ocean and everything else that makes up the natural world. That's Physics. Physics controls almost everything, but it doesn't control people's minds.'

'That sounds like magic at the most fundamental level,'

Meenakshi said. 'There are the principles of Alchemy and spells and incantations, but when you strip away the trappings, all it needs is ...'

'Thoughts,' Kalban finished.

'Thoughts,' said Chitralekha. 'Exactly. You can light a fire with your thoughts. Prehistoric humans didn't have even a fraction of the magical ability that people have today, but their need to have something to believe in was far greater. Physics already existed, but their belief put the Physics in a body and gave it will.'

'The Sun God and the Rain God.'

'The Sun God and the Rain God. Yes. And the Four Winds and the Ocean, the Lord of Spring and the Summer Queen. Once they'd set up their deities of nature, they started asking other questions. So you have the Goddess of Truth and the Goddess of Speech and the Dark Lady of Vengeance. And, eventually, the Sprites and the Dancers and djinn and every other class of immortal being.'

'What happens if people stop believing?'

'Nothing.' Chitralekha shrugged. 'Immortals don't die, by definition. They *do* lose their power, if nobody believes in them. Nothing happens in the real world because Physics is still Physics, but it dissociates from the body of the god concerned.'

'If Meenakshi's right ...'

'If Meenakshi's right, I can't help you.'

'You're a Celestial Dancer!'

'I'm not a Celestial Philosopher. I know the history, but I don't know what these people are doing with their experiments in belief and I have no idea how to stop it. Rambha herself couldn't help you with this. Besides, we don't even know yet that that's what it is. We have to confirm it. If Meenakshi's right, I'm going back to make a report.'

'Make a *report*?' Kalban threw his hands up. 'We have a gang of lunatics—'

'A *possible* gang of lunatics,' Chitralekha corrected.

'Very well, a *possible* gang of lunatics who are possibly creating an *im*possible nightmare monster, and you're going back to make a *report*?'

'That was my mission brief,' Chitralekha said. 'I'm here to reconnoitre.'

'Is your mission brief all you care about?'

'Don't get self-righteous with me. You've been quoting the Inter-Realm Accord at me since I got here. *Those* are the terms of the Inter-Realm Accord. If I've established that something is above my pay grade, I have to go back and make a report, on pain of having my pass revoked. I can't stay here and help you. I'm not afraid of what your friend's nightmare monster might do to me, but I *am* afraid of the Inter-Realm Liaison Bureau. There's even more paperwork at our end than there is here.'

'In any case,' added Meenakshi, 'we might not even need her help. Even if it is … what I think it is—it's still a creature, just like the griffons. There's no proof that it's malevolent. You're going to feel silly if you go charging in like an errant knight and it just wants to roll over and lick your hand.'

'Have some sense, Meenakshi! There's a reason this is forbidden magic! It's not a harmless little pet.'

Kalban turned to glare at the griffon, which was curled up in a corner worrying the edge of the carpet with beak and talons. It seemed to sense his gaze, because it looked up with an enquiring snuffle.

'I'm not saying it doesn't have the *potential* to be harmful,' Meenakshi said. 'But it hasn't actually done any harm, unless you count upsetting Avi as *harm*; and from what you've told me of him, he's the sort who always has to be upset by *something*. If not this, it would've been something else.'

'What about the God of Watchful Peace?'

'What about it? It's a statue. I don't suppose even the Priests of the Warlords really believe it means anything. Certainly nobody in the city does.'

'The Counsellor said there's been unrest.'

'This is Madh. There's always unrest. It's if the city is too *restful* that you know there's a problem. As for the God of Watchful Peace, I wouldn't be surprised if the High Priest did that himself.'

'And the people feeling tremors and vibrations around the Academy?'

'Oh, please. Everyone feels tremors and vibrations around the Academy on principle. It's like you, whenever you come into my study, looking around like you expect something with eighty legs and four mouths to burst out from behind a tapestry and eat you.'

Kalban edged away from the wall.

'Is there something with eighty legs and four—'

'*No.*'

'Look,' Chitralekha said, 'Meenakshi has a point—it hasn't done anything terrible yet. But,' she added to Meenakshi, 'that doesn't mean it's not dangerous. It's been doing a lot of things that shouldn't be possible in this realm. Maybe we've not seen the connection yet, but it can't be coincidence. We need to find out what it is.' She turned to Kalban. 'Do you want to speak to the Master Sorcerer?'

For a moment, it looked like Kalban was going to agree. Then he shook his head. 'Not until we know more about it or what it is. We can tell him when we have an answer to that.'

Then he flushed and averted his eyes from Meenakshi's too-knowing gaze.

'Really?' she asked. 'I thought I'd have to fight you over that. It isn't like you to pass up an opportunity to tell me how important it is to make sure somebody always knows about my hare-brained plans.'

'That only applies to *your* plans, not to mine. I make sensible plans.'

'So it's not because you're still upset with Father about—'

'That's enough,' Kalban said.

Chitralekha looked interested. 'Did you have a quarrel with the Master Sorcerer? You do know that's a stupid thing to do, don't you?'

'I did not have a quarrel with the Master Sorcerer,' Kalban growled. 'I'm his apprentice. Sorcerers don't quarrel with apprentices. They order them about.'

'I'm just giving you a friendly warning. I've seen his temper. There was this one summer, long before either of you was born—in fact, I think it was before he'd even met your mother, Meenakshi. It was a hot day, the rains were late ...'

'Is this the time for reminiscences?' Kalban asked.

'Isn't it?' Chitralekha shrugged. 'All right then. Somebody needs to speak to your crazy friend.' She responded to Kalban's outraged look with an apologetic shrug. 'That's what Meenakshi calls him.'

'Meenakshi is antisocial.'

'I'm a Celestial Dancer. We *invented* antisocial.'

'I thought what you invented was the opposite of antisocial.'

Before Chitralekha could retort, Meenakshi cut in. 'I'll speak to the Counsellor. You handle Avi and the High Priest.'

'What do you expect to learn from any of them?'

'We have a theory now. We only need proof one way or another. We look for signs ... verification.' Meenakshi turned to Chitralekha. 'Is there any way the Inter-Realm Sensors can confirm it for us?'

'We weren't seeing any individual spikes powerful enough,' Chitralekha said. 'But now we know why. There must be several of them, diffused, just like you said the residues were. One person couldn't do this, no matter how powerful. I can check up on the minor spikes, but over the course of an entire day nearly everybody is going to show a spike on the sensors at least once. We need a way to narrow it down.'

'Lure the thing out,' Meenakshi said promptly.

Kalban groaned. 'How did I know you were going to say that?'

'It makes perfect sense! We have to know who did it, or there's no point banishing it to the Inter-Realm or to Chaos or anywhere else. They can just make another. And Chitralekha's right, if it's a group of people working together, the individual magical usage spikes won't be large enough to pinpoint. We need to lure it out, force it to do something, and see whose usage spikes then.'

'There has to be another way.'

'There *is* no other way.'

'And how do you plan to make this work? Let's say you do manage to find it, which is by no means certain, how are you going to force it to do anything without it ripping you to bits? We have no idea how strong this thing is!'

'Actually,' Chitralekha said, 'we do have an idea how strong this thing is. I meant to tell you but you got caught up in your bickering. It's far stronger than either of you. It must be drawing its power from multiple sources. I expect it's tied to the people who created it ... What?' she asked Meenakshi, who was staring at her.

'Where would it get its power?' Meenakshi asked.

'From belief, isn't that what you said?'

'No, I said it gets its *existence* from belief. Where does it get its *power*? You said when people dreamed the gods into existence, the laws of Physics took a form.'

'She's right,' Kalban said. 'This thing is defying the laws of Physics. Do you think it could be drawing from the power of the people who created it?'

'If it is,' said Chitralekha, 'that might explain the—what did you say it was called? The Hidden Man?'

'Giving it its own power so it can stop drawing theirs,' Kalban breathed. 'And that might explain the anomalies. Magical power being consumed causes a reaction. That has to be it. But I still think there's something we're missing ... All right. Let's go with Meenakshi's plan and see where it takes us. She can go speak to the Counsellor, because he seems to like her enough to give her straight answers. I'll deal with everyone else here.'

'And I'll get the paperwork filed to monitor the sensors for individual spikes when you lure it out,' Chitralekha said brightly.

Kalban rolled his eyes and turned to Meenakshi. 'Dismiss her, then. She might as well file her paperwork.'

Meenakshi Dismissed Chitralekha with a snap of her fingers. As soon as she'd disappeared, Kalban said, 'No matter what you do, don't try to go after it. We have no idea what it can do. It's too dangerous, even for you.'

CHAPTER XIV

'The Free Bows have filed a complaint,' Asamanjas announced at the dinner table.

Meenakshi looked up. 'About the tortoise? There's no need to worry. The spell will wear off.'

'That's what I said in the official response. In any case, they have no grounds for action—the fool was trespassing on private property. He has to take the consequences. I just thought you should know, in case someone speaks to you about it.'

'That reminds me,' Kalban said, addressing himself to Paras. 'There was something I wanted to discuss with you.'

'What?'

'I spoke to the Free Bows yesterday. Two of them came to complain to me in person—and one was the First Bow.'

'Really? The First Bow?' Meenakshi asked. 'Why are the Free Bows so obsessed with this? It's not the first time one of them's found trouble by overstepping bounds.'

'Oh, they didn't come to complain because they wanted to *complain*. They wanted to pass on information without breaking their code of ethics—and, I suspect, without one specific client knowing that they'd spoken to me.'

'What did they want, then?' Asamanjas asked.

'They wanted to tell me who hired them—and why.'

'And?'

'They don't know the man's real name—and the client *is* a man. He came to them cloaked and hooded and refused to remove either the cloak or the hood.'

'That's not helpful. Not surprising, either. Nobody ever wants to show their face to a Free Bow.'

Meenakshi looked up. 'Don't Free Bows have an oath never to reveal the name of the person who hires them?'

Kalban scoffed. 'Never trust oaths, especially not oaths sworn by a hired thug. *Especially* not if you're hiring the thug to do something dangerous on your behalf. Anyway, they don't know the name, but he offered to pay them in Nectar.'

'What Nectar?' Meenakshi asked, even as Paras' brows drew together in a scowl and Asamanjas cursed.

'Don't be dense, Meenakshi,' Kalban said. 'The Nectar of Immortality.'

'Oh ... so she was right.'

'What?'

'She thought the Initiate who broke in had been taking Nectar. Something about his pupils being dilated. If I'd known, I would have used a Tertiary Modification for potential blood impurities, but he didn't come to any harm in any case.'

Kalban hoped Meenakshi's rambling about spell modifications would distract Asamanjas from her previous statement, but he should have known better. Scarcely had she fallen silent and returned her attention to her plate than he asked, 'Who is this *she*?'

'That's what the Free Bow told me, about the Nectar,' Kalban said before Meenakshi could respond. Asamanjas would see through the diversion, he had no doubt, but if Kalban could successfully turn the conversation, Paras might not. 'He said he refused, of course—the Free Bows aren't fools. They only deal in gold in any case; they don't even take land unless they're being hired by a head of state. But it appears that Chanura went behind the back of the First Bow.'

'That makes no sense,' Asamanjas objected. 'If the counterparty had already struck a deal with the First Bow, why would he give Chanura anything?'

'Maybe Chanura offered something the First Bow wouldn't. A willingness to enter the Palace grounds, for instance ... But I was thinking it might have something to do with the demigod who was smuggling Nectar—'

'Bringing Nectar into Madh for his personal use,' corrected Asamanjas.

'Without a letter from the Divine Physician,' Paras said. His expression was one Kalban had seen before. It meant he was not going to be budged by argument, storm or, as had happened on one memorable occasion, four runaway camels and an avalanche. 'Therefore smuggling.'

'Fine,' snapped Asamanjas, clearly recognising his brother's stubborn mood. 'He tried to smuggle Nectar. But what would a demigod want with the Free Bows?'

'Nothing, but we don't know where he was intending to supply the Nectar—oh, give it up!' Kalban said, when Asamanjas opened his mouth again. 'You know and I know that he wasn't bringing in four barrels of Nectar for his personal use. He must have been dealing with someone.'

'Why would he do that?'

'I have no idea.'

'You're both fools,' Paras grunted. 'Weren't you, Asamanjas, complaining to me only yesterday that several of the city's traders have had their goods transformed into djinn gold?'

'Djinn gold,' Kalban breathed, cursing himself for not having made the connection. The court bards of Melucha would get a year's worth of comic songs out of it if they heard. 'Of course. Djinn gold to pay the demigod.' He turned to Asamanjas. 'What happened to it? Did it disintegrate?'

'I told them to lock it out of sight for a few days, to be safe. It might still be there.'

'It might not. And transforming solid matter to djinn gold is one of the easiest transmutations. A first-year Alchemy student could manage it.'

'Wait,' Asamanjas protested. 'I know what you're alleging, but you have no proof! We can't go accusing a demigod based on mere suspicion.'

'We don't have to accuse him at all. It's none of our business what he does in the Inter-Realm. We only need to know who intended to buy the Nectar from him. If we find out who transmuted the gold ...'

'How can we do that?'

Kalban smiled. 'I think, for the first time in his life, the High Priest of the Sun God might be able to provide useful information.'

☩

The High Priest of the Sun God didn't look surprised to see Kalban.

'I thought you'd be back. Do you know anything about who profaned the God of Watchful Peace?'

'I'll find out—the sooner, if you can answer a question for me.'

'I doubt you have questions about Theology, and I don't know if I'm qualified to answer any other questions, but ask.'

'You know most of the other priests in the city, don't you? And they listen to you?'

'I know many of them,' the High Priest of the Sun God said cautiously. 'And there is ... mutual respect between us.'

'Particularly respect for *you*.'

'The Sun God has many devotees.'

'Good. Do you know the priests of ...' Kalban paused to leaf through the fifteen-page letter of complaint Nalini had had sent him, 'the God of the Black Sands?'

'Oh.' The High Priest's expression lost all guardedness, his nose wrinkling as though he had been bracing himself to hold back a flash flood with his bare hands and had encountered the runoff from a puddle instead. 'Black Sands ... One of the Lower Gods, isn't he? He hasn't been a major deity for centuries.' He shrugged. 'What do you want with *him*? If it's divine intervention you require, I can arrange it for you.'

'For a small fee, no doubt,' Kalban scoffed.

'A nominal fee ... You don't even need to pay upfront. I'm happy to take it in the form of a slight reduction in the taxes paid by the Sun Temple. After all, what is gold compared with the wellbeing of this great city? Shall we say a fifty percent reduction in taxes?'

'We can say a fifty percent increase in taxes if you persist in diverting the conversation. Do you know how mortals communicate with the God of the Black Sands? Only through his temple?'

'Most people use the temple. I suppose there might be private shrines, but they wouldn't open a line of communication unless they contained the black sands themselves—they're black because of ash,' the High Priest explained, seeing Kalban's bewildered expression. 'Volcanic sand from the Eastern Isles. The Temple has some, I know.'

'How easy is it to get?'

'Not very. Merchant ships won't carry it because its presence is reputed to attract cyclones and sea monsters. As far as I know, in Madh it's only available in the Temple of the Black Sands and the Academy.'

'The Academy?'

'In the science wing,' the High Priest explained. 'The Department of Geology.'

⚶

'There's something you should know,' Meenakshi said, 'before you go running off to the Academy to examine geological specimens.'

'I was going to go running off to the Inter-Realm Liaison Bureau to examine the border crossing records. Do I need to know it before that?'

'It would be as well.'

Kalban glanced at his foster-sister. Meenakshi seemed serious.

'All right, then. Tell me.'

'After the incident with the Free Bow who came in, I wrote to the Counsellor and asked for a favour. I wanted to know why he'd come—the Free Bow, I mean—and it would have done no good to ask *him*. He could just have lied.'

'So I've managed to teach you *something*,' Kalban muttered. 'What did the Counsellor say?'

'He just sent me a note.' Meenakshi waved a slip of paper at Kalban. 'He managed to track Chanura's movements in the week before he broke and entered. He says Chanura and the Free Bows' Commander-in-Chief were at Temple Square three days before that ... Talking to the God of Watchful Peace.'

'The God of Watchful Peace doesn't talk to anyone. He shivers shields and shatters spears.'

'That's what the Counsellor told his agent. But witnesses say there was a voice coming from the statue of the god's war elephant.'

'Witnesses? What witnesses?'

'Does it matter?'

For a moment, Kalban considered explaining to Meenakshi that there were perhaps two and a half inhabitants of Madh who were likely to overhear Free Bows plotting and then go and repeat the substance of the conversation to the Counsellor. Then he shook his head; this wasn't the time for exposition.

'Never mind. What did the voice say?'

'The Counsellor said his informant didn't tell him. I got the impression that he knew but he didn't want to tell *me*. Maybe he didn't think it was important.'

'That doesn't prove anything, then.'

'Not by itself. The next night, Chanura went back alone.'

Kalban let out a breath. 'It's circumstantial.'

'Of course it's not admissible evidence. The Counsellor's informants like their privacy.'

'Fine. Let's say it's true. Someone needed the Nectar of Immortality, which they bribed the God of Black Sands to smuggle across the border for them. They went for one of the obscure Lower Gods. He wouldn't have been getting much by way of votive offerings, so I'm sure the djinn gold was welcome. They also needed spies, and they tried to pay in Nectar because it's easy to make djinn gold—easier than getting normal gold, anyway. And Chanura only tried to get into your room after Avi had spoken to you.'

'The only reason anyone would need Nectar would be for a creature from the Inter-Realm.'

'There are other options ... But I don't think it's been reaching mortals. We would have known if there'd been a surge in the black market supply. If,' Kalban took a deep breath, 'if you're right about the other thing, if it's a ... a *Thoughtform* ...'

'That explains the Hidden Man. They don't exist, do they? They didn't until a few days ago. But if Avi knows—'

'We don't know that it was Avi!'

'Fine. If *someone*, the same someone who made the djinn gold and bought contraband Nectar and paid Chanura in it, knew about the legend—'

'It's frightening to a child. When I first heard it, I couldn't sleep for a week. I kept imagining the Hidden Man creeping up on me, moving from shadow to shadow to my bed and finally ...' He shuddered.

'Right. And if *someone*, naming no names, is scared of even perfectly normal things, he'd be terrified enough of the legend of Hidden Men to project his childhood fears onto the Thoughtform, maybe subconsciously. He might not have meant to do it.'

'Could it gain power this quickly?'

Meenakshi shrugged. 'According to the theory, it should take weeks to reach its current power.'

'The Nectar. That has to be it. Think about it. All the strangeness started after Black Sands was prevented from crossing the border with his supply—'

'Nectar acts as a sedative on the human mind ... and in a way, the Thoughtform *is* the human mind. Then I suppose security tightened. And they'd used some of their stock to pay Chanura—'

'Why Chanura?' Kalban said in frustration. 'That's what I don't understand. Someone made a bargain with the Free Bows. They agreed to pay a large amount of gold, from what I heard. Then why deal with Chanura at all, especially using their short supply of Nectar?'

'They might not have known it would be in short supply.'

'No, Black Sands had already been detained by then. They must have guessed that the customs officer would be more vigilant after that. They must have been desperate.'

'Maybe they wanted something the First Bow couldn't give them?'

'You're probably right. Couldn't, or wouldn't. The Free Bows don't tolerate threats to the order of the city.' Kalban muttered the last sentence under his breath. 'That has to be it. The client wanted something that would be a threat to the order of the city.'

'And the Free Bows refused, but later Chanura went back—or maybe he gave himself away and they called him back—and he agreed to do it for Nectar.'

'It's plausible. He wouldn't need gold. The Free Bows have plenty. But ever since your father took a hard line on the illicit trade, it's been near impossible to get Nectar in the city.'

'What do we do now?'

'Now,' Kalban said grimly, 'you are going to look into Thoughtforms and how to banish them, and I am going to speak to Avi.'

'Don't you think we should tell Father?'

'*No.*'

'If this is because you're worried—'

'It has nothing to do with my Tests!' Kalban snapped. 'The Master Sorcerer is the wrong person to help. It isn't pure magic that's going to banish a Thoughtform. It isn't created by magic, after all.'

'All right, and assuming I do find a way to get rid of it?'

'Just like you said. We'll lure it out.'

CHAPTER XV

Meenakshi felt a moment's trepidation when she looked at the stacks.

For magic so obscure, she had eschewed her personal collection. The Academy library, while extensive, was too full of bored clerks and chattering students for her comfort. Nothing would erase the memory of the day when she had been startled from a treatise on the five lesser magics by a small boy—a younger student, presumably—asking if she knew how to Summon a golem.

It wasn't that Meenakshi objected to Summoning golems in *principle*. That would be hypocritical, and Meenakshi wasn't a hypocrite. She merely objected to being interrupted when she was reading.

She had chosen instead the Governor's Library. Paras had declared it open to anyone in the city and it was, for that reason, seldom visited by anybody except him and Meenakshi. One of the few lessons of statecraft she had learnt from her father was that the best way to ensure that nobody is interested in something is to offer it to them for free. On days when Paras particularly wanted to be alone in the library, he sent out leaflets advertising an open lecture to be followed by an hour-long question-and-answer session.

The Governor's Library was empty of people, and the Governor's Library was *vast*. The collection, stretching from a rack of dusty—but, thanks to centuries of preservations spells, intact—codices acquired by the First High Loremaster before the foundation of Madh to a grimoire Meenakshi had ordered only a month ago, filled eighteen halls packed with floor-to-ceiling shelving. The library employed no fewer than fourteen clerks, but they tended to congregate at the acquisitions desk or in the reading room, leaving the labyrinth of books to itself.

The Chief Clerk and Keeper of Books (both positions held by the same harried individual) had asked Meenakshi half-heartedly if she needed any help. When she had replied with a firm negative, he returned to his chair with an air of relief.

Now, though, she was wondering if it wouldn't have been better to have accepted his offer. She didn't think he'd *know* where to find the information she needed—that was an arcane and dangerous branch of magic that hadn't been studied by anybody for at least two hundred years. But he might have helped her look.

She debated going back to get him but decided against it. The less he knew, the better Kalban would be pleased, and the less likely he would be to lecture Meenakshi about the indiscretion of revealing information to anyone who asked (or, in this case, who hadn't asked, and *that* would only prolong his diatribe).

She slipped silently through to Hall Nine, which had no windows, and went to a reading nook that was hemmed in by Metaphysics on one side and Modern Sociology on the other. She pushed aside the chairs and rolled back the carpet.

Only she and her father knew about the Summoning circle here. Kalban would disapprove, and her uncle would have the floorboards torn up and replaced, and then they'd have to go to the trouble of painting it again.

Meenakshi pushed aside *The Being in Relation to Cosmogony* and took out the lamps concealed behind it. She laid them around the circle, lighting them with a snap of her fingers before she stopped to think about whom she should Summon. Her first instinct was to fetch a Sprite. She was halfway through the spell before she realised that that too would result in a lecture from Kalban.

She Summoned Chitralekha.

'What?' Chitralekha demanded as soon as she'd materialised into the pentagram. 'I still have a dozen pages of forms to fill.'

'Never mind your forms. I need help.'

Chitralekha sighed. 'You know, *most* people in your position would be content to sit by the lotus pond and make the Palace jewellers miserable with unreasonable demands involving gold and rubies. But you have to meddle in affairs that are no concern of yours—and that are, moreover, no concern of *mine*. My part in this is done! I need to make a report. I can file a request for the sensors, but I can't help you.'

'I don't want you to help me get rid of the Thoughtform—if it is a Thoughtform. I just want help with research.'

'If your foster-brother finds out—'

'You can blame me. I'm used to his pontificating. Will you help me?'

'I'm not used to reading mortal scripts,' Chitralekha groused. 'They're cramped and crabby and they give you a headache. We do not use mortal scripts in our Realm. We communicate using the High Script, the Script of the Free Spirits, handed down ...'

'Handed down from generation to generation beginning with the First Lords of the Air,' Meenakshi finished. 'The foundation of Alchemy, Thaumaturgy and the High Arts. I've heard that speech too often to listen to it now.'

'Oh? From whom?'

'None of your business. What's wrong with you? You were willing to help—you were, if I remember correctly, eager to make one more conversion to turn Class III. What happened? Don't you want to be Class III anymore?'

Chitralekha looked around, and said, 'Do one of those noise-muting things.'

Meenakshi put a bubble of vacuum around them. 'Now tell me.'

'This sort of Thoughtform has been created once before—Urvashi told me the story. It was one of her conversions. A solo conversion and it took her straight from Class III to Command Group A.'

'Good. Did she tell you what to do about it?'

'She didn't do anything about the Thoughtform. She made sure the sorcerer concerned didn't try that particular trick again. Or any trick. I'm told that took some doing.'

'What happened to the Thoughtform?'

'The Fifth High Loremaster of Madh happened to it.'

'The Fifth High Loremaster?' Meenakshi's eyes widened in a sudden flash of understanding. 'He turned it into the phoenix!'

Chitralekha smiled. 'Very good.'

'That's why the phoenix really *is* a phoenix, and every bit as large and aggressive as the stories say. If he'd just used Alchemy it would have been—I don't know—a sparrow with a tolerance for high temperatures. How did he do it?'

'I have no idea. But he was powerful, Meenakshi. So are you, but he was far older and far more experienced.'

'It doesn't matter,' Meenakshi murmured. 'Magic couldn't have had anything to do with it. You said yourself they're not *created* by magic. We just need to understand what he did.'

'You can't be thinking of trying to handle this yourself.'

'Of course not. You and Kalban are going to help.' Meenakshi snapped her fingers, making the bubble dissipate. 'Come!'

'Wait! Where are we going?'

'Hall Four, Section XXXII. That's where the Fifth High Loremaster's writings are. You'll have to help me. I'll never get through all of them myself. He might have been a brilliant sorcerer but he was a rambling writer.'

Meenakshi wove her way through the shelves to Hall Four with Chitralekha following her, protesting all the way.

'Look,' Meenakshi said at last, 'I Summoned you, and if you don't want to do this, I'll Dismiss you. No hard feelings. But don't you think this will take you to Class III? How long are you going to have to wait for another chance if you let this one go?'

'A long time,' Chitralekha admitted. 'Decades. Now that there are Sprites on the waiting list too ... All right, I'll help you.'

'Here we are.' Meenakshi stopped in front of a rack. 'We'd better get the originals, hadn't we? The translations might have missed something.' With a glance in the direction of the reading room to make sure none of the clerks was watching, she snapped her fingers. Several scrolls and four codices floated off the shelf. 'We can take them to the nook in the back.'

⚛

'I have it.'

Meenakshi looked up from her reading. 'Does he say anything about how he did it?'

Chitralekha pushed the codex across the table at her, earning a hissed, 'Be *careful*. That's eight hundred years old.'

'And I'm even older. Read it.'

Meenakshi skimmed the first page. 'A Discussion of the Dark and Mystical Art of Giving Life to Thoughts ... power that we still cannot comprehend ... cannot be contained ... the direction an idea will take is unpredictable ... This is useless!'

'Keep going.'

Meenakshi flipped over a couple of pages. 'Significant Enquiry into the Allied Fields of Philosophy and Cosmogony ... the Nature of Sentience and Sense of Self ... this is just as bad ... oh, wait. It does get interesting.'

'I told you.'

Meenakshi studied the page for a while. 'I see how he did it ... It's going to be harder for us, though. If this is accurate, the Thoughtform *then* was created by a single determined individual. That's ... insane. How determined was he?'

'Why do you think Urvashi could bypass five levels? He wasn't powerful—not magically—but he was dedicated.'

'All right.' Meenakshi closed the book. 'We can do this. I'm going to find the Counsellor. I need to ask him something, and then I'll speak to Kalban. Are you going to help us or not?'

'You don't understand.'

'No, I do. Better than you think. You're frightened of what it might do to you. Your power comes from belief, just like the Thoughtform.'

'I'm not frightened of what *it* might do to me.' Chitralekha drew a breath. 'I'm ... concerned ... about what *they* might do to me, whoever created the Thoughtform.'

'I wouldn't worry. Everyone in the kingdom believes in Dancers—and enough people saw you that day. A few philosophers aren't going to make a dent in a belief held by millions.'

'You'd be surprised. But I'll come. I have to try. Besides,' Chitralekha added with a wry smile, 'you'll need me. The Fifth High Loremaster couldn't have done it without Urvashi, either.'

'Do we need anyone else? We don't know how many people might be involved. Should I Summon a Sprite?'

'I would ask which Sprite you're intending to Summon, but ... No. I can deal with this.'

'All right. Come.' Meenakshi paused. 'Don't do anything ... unnatural ... in the Counsellor's office. It bothers him.'

'I wouldn't dream of it.'

Meenakshi put the rest of the books back on the shelves and turned to lead the way out, but paused as the sound of voices floated into the room. She held up a hand to keep Chitralekha from moving.

'What?' asked the Dancer. 'You're so reclusive that you don't want to run the risk of meeting another person?'

'As a matter of fact, yes,' whispered Meenakshi, 'but that's not the point. Hardly anybody comes here.'

'Students of magic?'

'Students and professors all use the Academy library. It's very good and it's right *there*. The only reason to come here is—'

'If you *don't* want to meet people,' Chitralekha finished. 'Can you make us invisible?'

Meenakshi stared at her. 'Of course I can't make us invisible. Do you have *no* conception of how magic works? Even if I were to use a cloaking spell, the fundamental principle of—'

'Shhh! They're coming.'

Chitralekha pulled Meenakshi aside, hustling her behind a shelf just as several pairs of footsteps entered the room.

'Here,' came the voice of the Chief Clerk. 'Hall Four. This contains the personal writings of the Loremasters. I must urge you to be careful, as some of the manuscripts predate the founding of the city and have somewhat *aggressive* preservation spells.'

'Thank you,' said a voice that tickled the edge of Meenakshi's memory. 'I will exercise caution.'

She knew she had heard it before—and recently.

'Datta,' came Chitralekha's almost-soundless murmur in her ear as the Chief Clerk's footsteps receded.

'The writings of the Fifth High Loremaster,' said Datta. 'Do you know where they are?'

'Yes, here,' came another, entirely unfamiliar voice. Footsteps approached the stacks where Meenakshi and Chitralekha had been. Two people, or three? Meenakshi couldn't tell. 'Do you really think this will work?'

'Easily,' said Datta, with casual contempt. 'People are the same. Then. Now. Eight hundred years in the future they'll still be the same, a flock of frightened sheep.'

'If it needs magic though,' said the second voice, hesitantly, 'we might not be able to manage it. The Fifth High Loremaster *was* a very powerful sorcerer. Perhaps we should report this to the Master Sorcerer and ask him to help us—'

'I haven't worked this hard to go running to Paras now!' snapped Datta. 'He will learn—this city will learn—that there are more powerful things than magic. The Fifth High Loremaster knew that. It's a shame his successors don't. Now find the book. I believe it's called *Musings on the Applications of Philosophy*. It's very rare.' Datta made an odd explosive noise that, Meenakshi guessed, signified frustration. 'Scribes fall over themselves to make copies of his works on Summoning and Alchemy, and nobody realises that his most important work of all has nothing to do with magic.'

'Have you read it?' That was a third voice. Three people, then.

'No,' came the grudging admission. 'It's very difficult—*very* difficult—to get. This may be the only surviving complete copy. If we can find it.'

Meenakshi glanced down at the title of the codex before clutching it closer. She looked at Chitralekha, whose upraised finger warned her not to speak. They stayed where they were, listening to Datta and his two companions pull books off the shelves.

They worked without a sound other than the occasional muffled yelp when a book was handled too roughly and the spell on it sent a deterrent jolt up someone's fingers.

'It's not here,' one of the voices said a few minutes later.

'Look again. It must be here.'

'I'll bring the Chief Clerk,' offered the third voice, and the feet of its owner hurried away in the direction of the Acquisitions Desk.

'I wouldn't put it past them to have hidden it,' Datta muttered.

'If you don't mind my asking,' said his companion, in the sort of hesitant voice that said he was quite sure Datta *would* mind, '*why* can't we go to the Master Sorcerer? I know there'll be trouble, but he'll *have* to help. It's his job.'

'What have I always told you about the power of the human mind?'

'The power of the human mind exceeds every other power known to mortals,' was the response, in the singsong intonation of a memorised lesson. 'It has no limits, as Alchemy does. It has no laws, as Mathematics does. It can create or distort reality.'

'Precisely. This may be our only chance to *prove* that. Do you understand what this could mean to us *all*? There'll be no more tyranny of magic—'

Datta stopped talking abruptly. A moment later, Meenakshi heard people enter the room. She risked a quick peek around the side of the shelf. The Chief Clerk, with someone she thought was one of Avi's classmates in Applied Philosophy. Another of the students was standing with Datta.

At Chitralekha's insistent tug on her arm, she withdrew her head.

'*Musings on the Application of Philosophy,*' said Datta. 'I can't find it.'

Meenakshi could almost hear the Chief Clerk shrug. 'It ought to be there. I can check the catalogue, if you want, but it'll take some time.'

'Could anyone have taken it?'

'The Governor's daughter came in some time ago. It's not the sort of thing I'd expect her to read, but it's possible. She's probably in Hall Nine, that's where she likes to sit. We can go and ask. I'm sure she'll be happy to pass it to you when she's done.'

'That won't be necessary,' said Datta. 'Thank you.'

'All right ... Let me know if you need anything else, then.'

'You don't want it?' asked one of the students, in some surprise.

'I'm sure the Governor's daughter can be trusted to do the right thing... And if she doesn't figure it out on her own, I know who can suggest it to her.' There was something in Datta's voice that made Meenakshi shiver. 'Let's go. Everything is in good hands now.'

Meenakshi and Chitralekha saw Nalini before they saw the Counsellor. As they made their way down the corridor to the Counsellor's offices, Meenakshi heard someone calling her, and turned to meet Nalini's considering gaze.

Meenakshi suppressed a sigh. This was why one should always ignore it when one's name was called by a voice one didn't recognise.

'How can I help you?' she asked.

Nalini's eyes were on Chitralekha. 'I didn't approve any Dancers this morning.'

'I was Summoned,' Chitralekha replied.

Nalini shrugged. 'If you say so. I suppose you can control her, Meenakshi,' she went on. 'Even you, I hope, would have more sense than to Summon a Dancer you couldn't control. But that's not important now. I've been to see Kalban, but he's out. The Governor isn't admitting visitors, and I had rather not speak to him about this, anyway.'

'Has someone else been stopped at the border?'

'One of the Lake Guardians from the north.'

'Why was she entering the Mortal Realm here?' Chitralekha asked. 'Khand's the closest border crossing to the northern lakes.'

Nalini scowled at Chitralekha. 'How does it matter? She's entitled to cross where she wants, provided her paperwork is in order. I approved her forms myself, six days ago.'

'Around the time Black Sands was barred?'

'I ... Yes, I suppose so.'

'Let me guess. She had a chest full of Nectar and no letter from the Divine Physician?'

'She didn't know she needed one! This never happens in Khand. They're far more understanding of the differences between the mortal and immortal races. The problem with this city is that we have too much bureaucracy. I suppose ...' Nalini surveyed Meenakshi doubtfully. 'Can you speak to your father about it?'

'No,' said Meenakshi. She didn't elaborate further; reasons could be argued with. A simple and unexplained refusal was the quickest way to end a conversation.

Nalini didn't look disappointed. She probably hadn't expected much of Meenakshi. 'All right, then. If you see Kalban, tell him I want to speak to him. And *you*,' she added to Chitralekha, 'remember that if you're here for more than twenty-four hours at a stretch, you need a signed affidavit from your Summoner.' She turned to go, paused, and glanced at Meenakshi. 'I almost forgot. Kalban wanted to know about rogue Sprites who crossed the Border.'

'Yes?'

'Tell him there weren't any on record. But he's right about one thing. Urvashi and Rambha are both worried. They *think* there might be something djinn-class or higher in the Mortal Realm.'

'Nobody told me that,' Chitralekha protested.

'They think you're off the job, don't they? I don't suppose they even know you're here. Besides, it's not like they're going to reveal what they're thinking to a—what are you? Class I?'

'Class II.'

'Class II.' Nalini shrugged. 'So the only information you're privy to is the sensor readings. You couldn't Summon anyone more *useful* to help you, Meenakshi?'

Then Nalini really did leave, her laugh lingering in the air behind her.

'I do not like that woman,' Chitralekha muttered, as the door whispered shut behind Nalini and they made their way towards the Counsellor's office. 'So another one tried to smuggle Nectar.'

'They must be getting desperate.'

Meenakshi rapped on the door.

It was opened by one of the Counsellor's young assistants, who backed away without a word, allowing Meenakshi and Chitralekha to go through to the inner office.

The Counsellor looked startled to see them. 'That was quick. I barely sent the message off five minutes ago.'

'What message?'

'You're not coming from the Palace?'

'I was in the library. Why, is something wrong?'

'There's been another incident. Witnesses report seeing a griffon at the Academy last night.'

'That's all right, it would just have been—'

'Not one of yours. This one was reportedly the size of a fully-grown mountain lion, and, although my young assistants inform me that such a thing defies Physics, it could fly. It was also vicious and bad-tempered, and attempted to attack people.'

'And nobody could trap it?'

'My witnesses say it disappeared before it could touch them. They'd been drinking heavily, so they couldn't persuade the duty officer at the Arcane Zoology Authorisation Desk to believe them, and there's no sign of it this morning as far as I can tell.'

'But you think they weren't hallucinating?'

'I'm sure they weren't.'

'All right. I need to know something.' Meenakshi glanced at the door. It was shut. She lowered her voice all the same. 'I need to know the name of every person the Academy's Chair of Philosophy has spoken to, other than his regular classes, in the past month.'

CHAPTER XVI

'I don't know what you're talking about!' said Avi. 'And you think I'm involved in this insanity? That's ridiculous! Why would I have come to you in the first place? Why would I have endured your sister calling me crazy? Why would I have risked you looking into this affair if I were the one responsible for it?'

Kalban shot Meenakshi a warning glance just in time to prevent her from speaking.

As soon as she had told him what she and Chitralekha had heard in the library, he had guessed Avi wasn't guiltless. He had made the mistake of saying so aloud. Meenakshi, in proof of the fact that years of attempting to instil a semblance of diplomacy in her had been wasted, had been in favour of confronting him at once. It had taken considerable effort for Kalban to persuade her that they would get more information from Avi by being tactful, and especially by waiting until morning to speak to him instead of demanding explanations in the middle of the night.

'We don't blame you,' he said, hoping Meenakshi would be able to hold herself back from explaining in detail, with notes and supporting examples, how much she did blame Avi.

If what they suspected was true. He had to remember that. All they had so far was guesses. Kalban was certain they were right, he was certain perhaps based on Meenakshi's instincts even more than his own, but certainty wasn't proof.

'It's a difficult position to be in,' he went on. 'I understand. Of course I do. Many of them are your friends, and he—um— Datta, he's your professor. You didn't want to give them away. It's understandable, but we have to stop it. It can't go on.'

Avi kept on scribbling at his Summoning notes at the small desk in the Academy library, giving no indication that he'd heard Kalban. Kalban just managed not to grind his teeth.

'I can't help you,' Avi said at last.

Meenakshi opened her mouth again, and Kalban stopped her from speaking with another look. Not being oblivious to the nuances of human behaviour, he identified Avi's tone as *I CAN help you and I'm not unwilling but you'll have to give me an incentive.*

Kalban paused.

He knew how to conduct delicate negotiations, of course. He was Prince Heir of Melucha. He'd been talking his tutors into less homework before he'd reached his sixth birthday. But Avi was like no diplomat Kalban had ever met.

Avi was terrified in a way Kalban had never seen him before. He was afraid of something real and tangible, not a bogey he'd dredged up from the darkest depths of his own brain.

The brief moment Kalban let his attention wander was enough for Meenakshi to speak.

'If you tell us who instigated it,' she suggested, 'we can—'

'I don't know what you're talking about!' Avi snapped. Too quickly. Lying? Or just scared? With Meenakshi sitting opposite him, it could be either.

'You have the djinn spell backwards,' Meenakshi said.

'What? Have you been reading my notes?' Avi scooped up his papers and stuffed them into his satchel. 'Why were you reading my notes?'

'I wasn't. You have Nestor's *Summoning* open to the chapter on djinn. Nestor is very unsound on the subject of djinn. He's unsound on anything non-Yaunic. If you're really interested in Summoning djinn, I can recommend an informative series of essays—'

'Meenakshi!' Kalban hissed.

'Oh. Yes, of course. I'm sorry. Essays aren't important now. I was distracted by the book. I can't believe anybody would recommend that as a Summoning textbook, especially—'

'*Meenakshi.*'

'Right. The ... um ... the Thoughtform.'

Avi flinched. 'Don't say it. Not here. Identifying it gives it power. Thinking about it gives it power.'

'So it's true.'

'I don't *know.*' Avi pushed back his chair. 'I have to go. I'm sorry I can't help you.'

'Even if you don't *know*, you must *suspect*,' Meenakshi said.

'Meenakshi,' Kalban said, 'you're not helping.'

'It's true! He was in the Applied Philosophy Club. He knows everyone in it. He knows how they think. If anyone is going to know whose imagination could have conjured something that could meddle with the God of Watchful Peace and create a Hidden Man—'

'Hidden Man?' There was no mistaking the tremor in Avi's voice as he got to his feet. 'You're insane. That's just a legend.'

Kalban nodded at Meenakshi.

As Avi was about to walk away, she said, 'I saw you.'

Avi stopped short, his satchel falling from his hands. Papers spilled from it. The little bottle of ink rolled out, fortunately unbroken and with the cork still in. Kalban watched with an odd sense of detachment as it rocked back and forth, slower and slower until it was still.

'I don't know what you're talking about,' Avi said.

'Yes, you do. I was in the basement, and I saw you.' Kalban could never have managed Meenakshi's disinterested casual tone at such a moment. It was more effective than shouting would have been. 'You came after me—or you tried.'

Avi let out a breath. 'That was you?'

'Who did you think it could have been?' Kalban said, frustration getting the better of him. 'Avi, there's no getting out of it. I'd hoped—honestly, I'd hoped to sort this out without having to involve the Governor—but,' he added, at Avi's hopeful expression, 'this is serious enough that he'll have to know. It's not just mischief. It's not even petty crime. This is magic so dark and so dangerous that even the Fifth High Loremaster was frightened of it. Tell the truth.'

'It's not forbidden,' Avi said mutinously.

'No, of course it's not forbidden.' Meenakshi shrugged. 'You can't *forbid* people to *think*. You might want to do it, you might *try*, but it could never be enforced. It would be meaningless. But it's stupid to start something that you can't control—and nobody, *nobody* can control what will happen once you've created a spectre of fear. And if there's one thing the Master of the Academy likes less than student study groups doing homework together, it's student study groups doing stupid things together.'

Kalban would have remonstrated with her, but Avi looked as though he was about to crack. Apparently, some people did need the direct approach.

All the same, he couldn't let it pass without even a token protest. 'Meenakshi, be polite.'

'I had no idea,' Avi whispered. 'I had no idea it would turn into this.' He looked at Kalban, who felt a frisson of fear. 'You have to believe me. It was just supposed to be an experiment ... We didn't know if it was even possible. Kashyap said it would be tame ... like Alchemical beasts. Which of us hasn't tried that? *She* probably has an entire filing cabinet to herself at the Arcane Zoology Authorisation Desk. I didn't think this would be any different.'

'Does it stay in the basement?'

'Usually—yes—it can't leave by itself. I mean ... It's held in by the Academy's magic barriers. I suppose someone could lead it out, but we've never done that.'

'You've taken it around the lower levels of the city through the tunnels,' Meenakshi pointed out. 'I suppose that's why people have been reporting strange noises.'

'We needed to let it move. It was getting restless, cooped up in just that one room, and we didn't dare let it move around the rest of the Academy basements. Too many people. We weren't expecting *you* to be wandering around the tunnels.'

'Is there any way to unmake it?' Kalban asked.

'No,' Avi said in despair. 'We tried. We tried everything. Every spell and weapon we could think of, and nothing worked. Professor Datta had us try every single Dismissal in every book of Summoning we could find—'

'That's why you were reading Nestor?' Meenakshi demanded. 'To find a Dismissal? A *djinn* Dismissal from Nestor for this ... whatever it is that you've created? You must be desperate.'

'*Yes!*' Avi's voice was rising in his anger. The librarian glared at him.

Avi blushed and went on, more quietly, 'Yes. Yes, I am desperate. We've been feeding it Nectar to keep it quiet, but our supply's running low. It was running low when I came to you. That was why I came to you. The Master Sorcerer's experiments are famous. Kalban's lived with him for years, I thought he might have some idea of what to do. We have enough Nectar left to keep it calm for another six hours, maybe. After that there's no way to control it.'

'We won't need six hours,' Meenakshi said.

Avi looked at her. 'I know they say you're good, but even *you're* not that good. Kashyap's been trying for days.'

'*Kashyap's* been trying? What about *you*?'

Avi shrugged. 'I left the Applied Philosophy Club. I still ... I go down to help with ... with it once in a while, when it's getting rambunctious and they need another person, and I've been doing a bit of research, but ... that's it.'

Meenakshi looked appalled. 'That's *it*? You were part of the problem, and you just *left*?'

'I still help! I just ... didn't want to get in trouble.'

'You didn't want to get in trouble.'

'Meenakshi,' Kalban warned.

'What? You should be ticking *him* off, not me. You call me a sociopath, and even I know you don't do that.'

'Meenakshi, sometimes people have reasons for their actions that may not be immediately apparent to you. I'm not saying Avi wasn't a coward,' he went on, ignoring Avi's scowl. 'I'm saying we should withhold judgement until we know *why* he was a coward.' Kalban glanced at the librarian, who had shifted her attention to a student who had brought in her pet krait. 'You have your chalk, Meenakshi? Good, go behind that shelf and Summon Chitralekha. I have to talk to Avi and you're putting his back up.'

'I'm right here,' said Avi.

'Yes, you are.' Kalban turned to his friend. 'I understand. Meenakshi's overconfident and a bit of an idiot, so she has no idea why you'd be frightened enough to run from a problem of your own creation. I do. I understand, but the fact remains that you did it. The Master Sorcerer and the Master of the Academy are going to take an even dimmer view of this than Meenakshi. If you help us fix it, we *might* be able to persuade them that there is hope for you.'

'I'm sorry, am I interrupting something?' Chitralekha's voice broke in before Avi could give voice to any of the—judging by his expression—outraged responses that were floating through his head.

'Who is *she*?' Avi asked, eyes widening and mouth opening until he looked like a deranged sheep.

'Chitralekha, this is Avi. Avi, Chitralekha. Chitralekha, to answer your question, no. I was attempting to give Meenakshi a lesson in negotiating, but that can wait.'

'*That's* how you negotiate? That's nothing like how we do it. Judging by what I saw just now, our way of doing it is *far* more effective. I could give Meenakshi pointers about—'

'*No!*'

Meenakshi looked interested. 'Pointers about what?'

'No,' Kalban repeated before Chitralekha could answer. 'Nobody is giving Meenakshi pointers. That's exactly what we need, for her to start getting curious about how Dancers negotiate.'

'Have it your way. It was just a suggestion.' She looked around. 'Shouldn't we take this somewhere else? I wouldn't want to disturb the peace of the library.'

'We can find an empty Summoning room,' Kalban said, getting to his feet. 'Come.'

It didn't take them long to find a secluded place to talk. Once there, Chitralekha said, 'Meenakshi, I did what you wanted.' She produced a fistful of shimmering strips of paper, seemingly from thin air. 'Here are the readouts.'

'What are these?' Avi asked.

'Sensor readouts for everyone Professor Datta has spoken to recently—including the three of you, of course.'

'Of course,' Kalban said dryly.

'Meenakshi's charts are normal,' Chitralekha explained, showing them. 'Some minor spikes, nothing out of the ordinary. Kalban, yours, as I said earlier, are a little below your twelve-month average. You really should be practicing for Finals. The *rest* of them ...' She knelt, rolling the strips out flat on the ground. 'There were approximately two hundred people, including other teachers and students to whom he's been giving remedial lessons. Eighteen of those showed an uncharacteristic dip in the past three weeks.'

'How much of a dip?' Kalban asked.

'They're at less than a quarter the twelve-month average. Even during vacation time it doesn't drop below half. And there are no spikes when there should be spikes. Look at this.' She pointed at one of the strips. 'That's a practice session for the Free Magic Open Tournament. That should cause a spike to three or four times the thirty-day average, but it's barely even registered.'

'Whose is that?' Kalban squinted at the label, which was in High Script.

'That's Avi's,' said Chitralekha. 'These are all members of the Applied Philosophy Club, according to the Counsellor's information.' She glanced at Avi. 'Maybe you can confirm it for us.'

'No need,' said Kalban. 'The Counsellor doesn't make mistakes. All right, is there anything else?'

'Yes. Each of these dips,' she pulled aside a few, 'corresponds to one of the spikes we saw on the sensors.'

'Are they powerful enough to account for the spikes?' Meenakshi asked, leaning in.

'No, but I don't think that's how this works. It draws baseline power from the people who created it, which is why their output is low. The Academy is full of magical residues. They seep through the walls. That's where it gets the rest of its power. The dips must represent a moment when somebody, for lack of a better word, *imagined* new powers into existence for the ... Thoughtform.' Chitralekha indicated the bottom strip, which showed a flat line. 'That's Datta's. He's not a practitioner of magic. He does have minor variations in output but nothing that would be visible to a mortal.'

'But his belief still affects the Thoughtform?'

'I should think so,' Chitralekha said. 'But there's no way to know for certain.'

'I think so, too,' Avi offered. 'I mean, it did change with his thoughts even more than with ours, especially in the beginning. He may not be a sorcerer, but there's something about him ... When he wants something, he really wants it.'

'So just one person thinking something is enough to change it?' Meenakshi asked.

'In the first week, it was enough. Any of us could do things to it just by thinking of them. But as it grew more powerful, it took more effort. Two people, three, four ... We haven't been able to do it at all for the last three days. Maybe, if all of us could manage to focus on the same thing, but ... eighteen people, twenty-three if you count the professor and a few other non-practitioners in the club. It's impossible.'

'It fits,' Chitralekha said.

Meenakshi nodded. 'The Fifth High Loremaster said he managed to turn the Thoughtform into a phoenix by forcing the idea of the phoenix on the thoughts of the creator. But that was just one creator.'

'What do we do?' Kalban asked.

Meenakshi smiled. 'I have a plan.'

CHAPTER XVII

'You're insane,' Avi said, when Meenakshi finished explaining her plan.

'Do you have a better idea?'

'Avi's right,' Kalban said. 'It's dangerous. No matter what Avi wants us to believe, the Thoughtform wasn't conceived out of intellectual curiosity.'

'Why else would anyone do it?'

'Think, Meenakshi. They did it because they were frustrated, and frustrated people do stupid things! Because someone had an essay returned with no marks and orders to do it over. Because someone else was reprimanded before a full class and had ideas of petty revenge. Because someone wanted to attract attention and couldn't think of another way. Any of those things. *All* of those things. Do you realise what that means?'

'I'm sure you're about to tell me.'

'It's a Thoughtform. It draws its nature from its creators. If it was conceived in bitterness and anger, that's what's going to inform its temperament. It isn't gentle. It *couldn't* be gentle.'

'He's right,' Avi said. 'It isn't gentle.'

'Does anybody have a better idea?'

'No,' Kalban admitted. Avi gave a reluctant nod.

'Then we're doing this. If all it's known is frustration and bitterness and anger, we have to give it something else to think about.'

'We show it kindness?' Avi asked.

'By all means try it,' said Meenakshi, 'but that won't help. We can't solve the problem by buying it flowers. The Thoughtform was conceived in the grip of ... mainly frustration, I suspect, along with a little curiosity.'

'It had anger from Datta,' Kalban offered.

'With so many creators, it must be full of conflict, confusion ... and consequently more anger. We—or, to be precise, *you*—will try to give it reason.'

'I don't know,' hedged Avi.

'I do,' Meenakshi said. 'We're only going to have one chance. We have to be ready. Avi, go find everyone who was in the Applied Philosophy Club when the Thoughtform was created, including the people who got cold feet like you did, and make sure they're in the building. Were the students all residents?'

'Yes. Finals are soon. Everyone's going to be here studying—but I'll check. I don't know if I can get them all into one room, though.'

'That's all right. Just make sure they're in the Academy.'

'If they're not?'

'If they're not, we wait until they are. Don't bring them here, don't ask probing questions, don't do anything unusual. It's going to be difficult enough as it is to make sure they're all having the same ideas. We don't need curiosity about your motives intruding. When you've done that, meet us back here. You're going to lure it out for us.'

Avi hurried out.

'He's not going to run away, is he?' Chitralekha asked.

'I'll keep an eye on him,' Kalban promised.

'How?'

In response, Kalban went to the equipment cupboard and took out a mirror.

Meenakshi stared. 'You're going to *scry*? Isn't that a violation of privacy?'

'Of course it is, and Avi is free to file a complaint about it. Hadn't you better be getting ready for your part in this?'

Chitralekha glanced at her. 'I take it your part is going to be more than what you described to us just now.'

'If Avi knows what I'm planning, it won't work.'

'We're not trying to teach the Thoughtform reason, then.'

'Of course we're not. Something with passion and reason but no compassion? How do you think that would work?'

'Oh, we have those already. They're called djinn.' Chitralekha shrugged. 'And I take it the plan isn't to teach it compassion.'

'Kalban's right. If it was conceived in bitterness, that's going to be its defining trait no matter what we do. *We* can't turn it into compassion. Maybe its creators can, but we can't gamble on their intentions.' Meenakshi got to her feet. 'All right. The two of you keep an eye on Avi—'

'You can't leave her with me!' Kalban protested. 'You're her Summoner. I can't control her if she tries something!'

Chitralekha scowled at him. 'You still don't trust me? What's wrong with you? What have I done in the entire time you've known me to make you think I'm going to *try something*? Your friend is the one who helped *create* a creature nobody's seen since the days of the Fifth High Loremaster! And while I'm on the subject, is this really all there is to it? Smuggling Nectar, creating djinn gold, it's a lot of trouble to take for students out of bounds.'

'I'm sure there's more,' Kalban agreed. 'But at the moment, this is what we can deal with. Meenakshi, don't be long.'

'Don't worry.'

Meenakshi felt the Academy changing around her as she hurried through the corridors. It had been the painted marble of a Yaunic temple when she had entered earlier, floors polished until she could see her face in them. Now it was dark and forbidding.

It was as though the spell on the Academy was reacting to her intentions.

The spell had always fascinated her. It was old magic—old, but not ancient. Ancient magic was the simplest of all forms of magic, and therefore the most difficult to understand and next to impossible to control. Old magic ...

Old magic was seldom as untouched as the spell on the Academy appeared to be. It felt as though nobody had meddled with the spell since it was first laid, which astonished her. Magicians had all the curiosity of cats without the caution. If there were a spell book with 'DANGEROUS MAGIC DON'T TRY THIS ARGHHHH' written across the cover in letters of blood, one could bet that one young sorcerer per month would get third-degree burns trying to see what it did.

But now wasn't the time to think about that.

Meenakshi went back to her apartments for the notes she needed. It took some digging, since Illusions were dealt with in introductory Theory of Magic classes—or, if you were the daughter of the Master Sorcerer, in bedtime reading when you were four. At last, she located them, between a stack of basic spell books and a sheaf of marked essays.

She gathered the pages.

As she was about to leave, she heard a faint squawk from her bedroom, and remembered the griffon. On impulse, she went in, whistled to it, and led it out. The griffon had seemed to frighten the Thoughtform the last time, after all. It might be helpful again.

By the time she got back to the Academy, Avi had returned. He wore a distinctly sulky expression and Kalban the look of long-suffering grimness that preceded a lecture on common sense.

'Kalban's crazy friend *did* try to run away,' Chitralekha said as soon as she saw Meenakshi.

'I'm not crazy!' Avi snapped. 'And I wasn't trying to run away. I wanted to take a walk to settle my nerves.'

'You wanted to take a walk to the public stables and buy a swift horse to take you back to Melucha,' said Chitralekha. 'I can read mortal intentions. I can tell when you're fleeing and I can tell when you're lying.'

'He's here now,' Kalban said. 'It doesn't matter. Meenakshi, do we need the griffon? We can't make a habit of letting it run loose around the Academy. What if it leads the others here when we send it back to the vaults?'

'We don't have to send him back,' Meenakshi pointed out, scratching along its neck where feathers turned to fur. The griffon opened its beak to screech enthusiastically, but a sharp tap quieted it before it could. 'He won't get in the way. He's tame.'

'We'll discuss it later,' Kalban muttered. 'There's no time for this now. Let's go.'

⚜

'How do you see it?' Meenakshi whispered to Kalban as they stole down the basement stairs.

Kalban squinted. 'A little too much light, but that's all.'

Meenakshi let out a breath. It was reacting to her intentions, then. Would that affect the Thoughtform? There was only one way to know.

'We should have brought Nectar,' Avi said, his voice a little too high to be comfortable listening. 'That's the only thing that calms it.'

'No,' Meenakshi said. 'That's been the problem all along. We need everyone clear-headed. Which way?'

'To where we usually ... meet it? Here.' Avi led the way through the basement. He was vibrating with terror.

Kalban was nervous, too; he was trying not to show it, but the way he started every time the griffon's talons clattered too loudly on the floor gave him away. Chitralekha was the calmest of them. Her scarves floated serenely in a breeze nobody else could feel.

'Are we getting closer?' she asked.

Avi squeaked.

Something stirred in the shadows. Meenakshi stopped, stilling the griffon with a hand to its head.

'He'll be expecting me to have something,' Avi whispered. 'An offering. We never come empty-handed.'

'Can it talk?'

'He's talking now,' hissed Avi. 'Don't you hear him?'

Meenakshi glanced at Kalban, who shrugged, and at Chitralekha. The Dancer shook her head.

'We don't hear anything,' said Kalban. 'Maybe only those who created it can hear it. What's it saying?'

'*I can speak.*' The murmur was sibilant, seeming to come from everywhere and nowhere. '*It's just … easier … not to. I've seen you before.*' The shadows stirred, closer, and a chill crept up Meenakshi's spine. '*What brings you here?*'

'We want to talk to you,' Meenakshi said. 'Show yourself.'

'*I think not.*' The words were followed by laughter that echoed off the walls. The shadows lengthened, seeming to wrap themselves around its source. '*You made a terrible mistake. You came here thinking you could finish me.*'

'We have to go,' Avi said.

'Be quiet,' snapped Meenakshi.

'We have to *go*.'

The ground under them trembled, faint cracks spiderwebbing across the floor.

'Meenakshi,' Kalban said, and she knew he was seeing the cracks as well. Either they were real, or ... 'Tell me you know what you're doing!'

'This can't be happening!' Chitralekha said. 'There are protective spells on the Academy buildings. It's impossible to break them. *This can't be happening!*'

'No spells are unbreakable,' Meenakshi replied. 'He's not a creature of the Inter-Realm. I think he doesn't like it. They opened a portal to try to push him through—'

'*I opened the portal!*' came the Thoughtform's voice.

'Then why didn't you go through it?'

'He wouldn't have held together.' Chitralekha was looking into the shadows. Perhaps she could see the Thoughtform. 'I can sense it. He's cracking at the seams. There's too much—too many wild rambling ideas from too many minds—stuffed in. He couldn't have held together under the buffeting of Chaos.'

'It's his creators,' Kalban said, understanding. 'They might have had clear intentions when they made him, but since then they've been panicking. Nobody's being rational.'

'They're terrified,' Meenakshi said.

Avi proved her point by letting out another frightened squeak. The shadows darkened, twisting.

'And their fear gives it power. You always think a thing is worse, bigger or stronger or angrier, when you're afraid of it.'

The air tingled, growing warm.

'Meenakshi,' hissed Kalban.

Kalban was seeing and feeling the same things she was. Avi too? Perhaps. Either the thing was controlling the spell on the Academy, or her plan was working. Maybe both.

But she needed more time.

Shadows were only frightening if there was light to cast them.

Kalban seemed to have the same thought, because he snapped his fingers, snuffing out both his and Avi's torches. The room was plunged in utter darkness, broken only by the faint pearlescent glow of Chitralekha's skin. There was no knowing where the Thoughtform was.

'We're going to die here,' Avi moaned.

The floor and walls were thrumming.

'Do you think it can affect the rest of the Academy or only the basement?' Meenakshi asked.

'You think it can affect *everything*?' Avi asked in horror.

'*Now* it can,' Kalban said in an undertone. 'Is that what you're going for? Frightening him into giving it more power?'

'Trust me.'

Kalban shrugged. 'Might as well do it properly, that's all I'm saying.' He raised his voice. 'Avi, maybe it can absorb magic from the residues in the Academy and throw blasts of it at us.'

'You don't do things by halves, do you?' called Chitralekha, seizing Meenakshi's wrist and pulling her behind a pillar just in time to avoid a flare of energy. 'How is this even working? Avi said one person couldn't affect it anymore!'

'Because they were trying to contain its powers.' Meenakshi peered out from behind the pillar. 'Giving it powers is easier.'

Kalban darted across the passage to join them. 'What now?'

'*This.*' Meenakshi whistled to the griffon.

She didn't see it take flight, but she heard the clatter of claws and the whoosh of wings and the screech that echoed back and forth until it sounded like there were at least fifty eagles in the room.

She knew the griffon was harmless, and Kalban and Chitralekha knew it was harmless, but Avi didn't.

She sensed the moment when the Thoughtform reared back from the griffon, for an instant as frightened of it as Avi was. There was a loosening in the air.

Meenakshi found the spell on the Academy and gave it a tug.

For a moment, nothing happened, and she thought she hadn't managed it. Then white light filled the room. The walls shimmered, seeming to collapse in on themselves. A grey mist descended.

When it lifted, the floor was tiled in polished stone and the walls and ceiling painted a pale, neutral cream. In the corner of the room was a man, a short, balding, nondescript man.

'Is this what the Academy really looks like?' Kalban asked, gazing around the room.

'Yes, but never mind that. *Get him* now! He has no power but it won't last long.'

Kalban hadn't been taught to be his own last line of defence in a court crawling with assassins for nothing. In less than a minute, he had the man in what looked like a painful hold.

'What do we do with him?' Kalban grunted.

'Are you going to lecture me if I open an unauthorised Inter-Realm portal now?'

'Do it!'

'Take him,' Meenakshi told Chitralekha, opening a portal in front of them with a snap of her fingers. 'I'm sure Urvashi and Rambha will know what to do about him.'

'I'm sure they will.'

As soon as Chitralekha and the Thoughtform had vanished, Meenakshi released her hold on the spell. The basement plunged back into its accustomed dank gloom.

'Well,' Kalban said, 'I think we can make a case to Asamanjas for you keeping the griffon as a pet. Just this once.'

CHAPTER XVIII

eenakshi waited a couple of hours before she Summoned Chitralekha again. Kalban, instead of mopping his brow, strewing rose petals, or showing any other sign of the relief that Meenakshi would have considered the appropriate response to removing the incipient threat, had spent the time staring out of Meenakshi's study window as though he expected a maelstrom to appear in the middle of the Pool of Lotuses. Even Chitralekha's confirmation that the Thoughtform was now safely in the hands of those who would be able to solve its problems did nothing to lighten his gloom.

She said as much.

'Of course he's still worried,' Chitralekha responded. She glanced at Kalban, and then her eyes flitted to Avi, who had been so still that Meenakshi had forgotten he was present. 'This isn't over. Taking care of the Thoughtform isn't enough.'

Meenakshi shrugged. 'It explains everything. Almost. It doesn't particularly explain the God of Watchful Peace, because as far as I can tell, the Thoughtform only did what they wanted it to, whether consciously or not, and ... Still. People are strange. Their actions are inexplicable.'

'One month,' Chitralekha murmured to Kalban. 'Just let me have her for *one* month. She's bright. She'll learn quickly.'

'No, thank you.' Kalban looked at Meenakshi like he wanted to whip out a book of political science and a blackboard. 'Meenakshi, *think* for a moment. All this trouble didn't happen because a few Philosophy students were bored. You know what bored students think up? Ways to pass exams without studying, or to have their term papers magically written for them. Left to *them,* the Thoughtform would have spent its time in the library writing Alchemy dissertations.'

'What are you saying?'

'Let me,' said Chitralekha briskly. 'I've had aeons of practice dealing with genius idiots. Meenakshi, Datta preyed on his students' fears to make the Thoughtform. He did, you said it yourself. They may have thought it was their own idea but we've seen just how effectively a thought can be planted.'

'It was a dry run,' Kalban explained.

Avi squeaked. 'You mean there are more Thoughtforms? I never heard of any others.'

'Not yet. But there will be more Thoughtforms in the city soon, if there aren't already. He's trying to manipulate the city. The High Priest of the Sun God thought so. I should have listened to him. The man has an unhealthy fondness for not paying taxes, but he knows the mob. You sow fear in their minds, slowly, with a moving statue here, trade goods turned into djinn gold there, weird noises and mutterings and rumblings ...'

'Not in Madh,' Meenakshi protested. 'People are used to strange things. The God of Watchful Peace didn't frighten anyone.'

'Yes, it would take some doing. In any other place, the God of Watchful Peace might have been enough. Here, it just aroused interest. But eventually people would have started to worry, to be afraid.'

'The strongest fears don't come from superstitious idiots starting at noises and calculating the trajectories of flying birds.' Chitralekha tossed her head. 'They'd cause bogeys and gremlins and minor annoyances you could swat away. But when people who aren't normally fearful learn to be afraid, they do it with *everything* they have. Their fears are stronger. Whatever comes from them will have more power. That's how it works.'

'Still.' Meenakshi scratched the griffon's head. 'You said it was people's beliefs that created every class of Immortal being. Datta will frighten everyone in the city and make some new species of yaksha or something and it'll be taken across the border and taught how to behave in civilised society. End of story.'

'Not quite. Every class of Immortal being that you know now was created by *belief*. There was a little fear, fear of that which wasn't understood, but the act of creation quelled the fear and that's why not even yakshas and djinn are uncontrollable. They were made in fear, yes, but also in reason and the belief that higher forces could be explained and comprehended. If Datta and his co-conspirators succeed in making the people of Madh create something in their terror of the unknown, it will be far worse. Your spells won't be able to snap them out of it.'

'The First Bow must have guessed something of what he plans,' Kalban muttered, 'or he wouldn't have involved me. But what do we do?'

Chitralekha's eyes gleamed. 'We have to stop him. And there isn't much time. There's an undercurrent of fear in the city now that I wasn't sensing a few hours ago. It's growing stronger. It'll be out of control soon.'

'Why would fear suddenly ratchet up?' Meenakshi asked. 'Nothing's happened in the last few hours.'

Chitralekha looked at Kalban.

'Let me handle it,' said Kalban in response to her look. 'Meenakshi, something *has* happened, something far more alarming than a full choir of disembodied voices. For as long as anybody can remember, the Royal Academy has shone in golden splendour in the heart of Madh. Nothing changed that, not the Eight Djinn, not the Meru Incident, *nothing*. Today, for a short time, the Academy looked like a government building designed by an architect in the middle of a minimalist phase. I'm sure you can understand why this might upset people.'

'It was just a spell!'

'Non-practitioners don't understand what that means. Meenakshi, *I* was scared, and I knew it was a spell and you were holding it! Imagine how terrifying it must have been for everyone else! I know you had to do it. But it probably frightened people more than everything else that's happened put together.'

'That must have been Datta's plan all along,' added Chitralekha. 'He knew Avi was Kalban's friend. He would have known it would end in you doing something ... entertaining. We have to stop him before he can carry out the rest of it.'

Kalban shook his head. 'Even if I have the City Guard arrest Datta and all his friends, that won't help. He's loosed the demons. We can't arrest everyone in the city of Madh. It won't take much to set it off, now.'

'We have to give them something else to think about,' said Meenakshi. 'That's the only way.'

'What are you talking about?'

'Everyone's afraid. There's strength in the beliefs of a mob. So we give them another spectacle, bigger than the Academy, one they'll *believe*. Shock them out of the fear and it'll *go*. Avi's professor won't be able to bring it back after that ... Certainly not from whichever distant land Father exiles him to.'

'How are we going to do that?'

⚜

Asamanjas was in Paras's study. For a moment, Kalban considered asking to speak to his Master alone, but in the end he decided he might as well tell them both at once and get it over with.

He kept his explanation short, and waited for the questions.

To his surprise, none came. He looked up to see Paras and Asamanjas exchanging a glance of bemusement.

'What *is* it with you people?' Asamanjas asked, but his question was directed at his brother. 'It's like an epidemic. All I ask is that you tell me before Meenakshi's time comes. Then I can arrange to take a short holiday at the other end of the world. Perhaps there is an active volcano I might explore, or a new species of venomous cobra waiting to be discovered.'

'I thought Kalban might prove to be the exception,' said Paras. 'He's always so infernally *sensible*.'

'That makes it even worse. It's the stored-up rebellion of ... what, five years? Six? Your last major act of rebellion was running away from Melucha, wasn't it, Kalban? How long ago was that?'

'If you don't mind my asking,' said Kalban faintly, 'what on earth are the two of you talking about?'

'Your Tests,' said Asamanjas. 'I told my brother not to spring them on you without warning. But does he ever listen to me? You owe me a string of pearls for that, by the way, Paras.'

'You were wagering on what I would do?'

'That,' said Paras, 'is neither here nor there. So this what's-his-name, Datta, you think he intends to create Thoughtforms across the city? Why would he do that? And what makes you think that benighted maniac and a gaggle of disgruntled students will able to create so many of them? They won't be stable. Even if Datta somehow manages to make them, he doesn't have the smallest hope of controlling them.'

Asamanjas drew in a deep breath. 'Kalban, I take it you have a plan. You might want to share it before I start panicking. I doubt even Paras and the Master of the Academy between them could fend off dozens of nightmare creatures rampaging uncontrolled through the streets.'

'We *think* he's going to do something tonight to bring it to a head—to *create* the creatures. Avi's gone to find out what. If we stop him and break the tension ...'

'Right,' said Asamanjas. 'As soon as Avi finds out what Datta and his associates have planned, Paras will go and—'

Paras cleared his throat.

'What?' asked Asamanjas irritably.

'I don't think, actually, that I'll do anything.'

Kalban and Asamanjas both stared at him.

'You're not serious?' Asamanjas said. Kalban would have

echoed the sentiment if he hadn't been struck temporarily speechless. 'You're just going to *let* this happen?'

'Kalban's handling it.'

'No.' Asamanjas spoke in the weary tone of one who knows he's going to lose the argument, because he's been losing the same argument for years, but is going to have it anyway. 'We've talked about this, Paras. You can't just abdicate responsibility for things that don't interest you. That's why people like Datta think they can take over.'

Paras scoffed. 'Datta thinks he can do my job, does he? He would be cowering in a corner at the sight of the first rogue yaksha. There would be a lot more rogue yakshas if Datta were in charge.'

Kalban, still mute with horror, had to admit the truth of that. The knowledge that the Master Sorcerer didn't like disturbances did far more to keep the peace than all the burly spearmen the Captain of the Guard could produce. That seemed to him an excellent reason for Paras to come and keep the peace now.

'Yes, I know,' said Asamanjas. 'But it's not enough, Paras. You have to be *seen* to be in charge. The Maharaja knows why we need you here—I know—and I daresay even Nalini knows, which is why she hasn't yet tried to depose you. Many people *don't* know, and it must seem to them that there's a vacuum in power just asking to be filled.'

'Let's discuss all that later,' replied Paras. That was more interest than Kalban had ever heard him express in the subject. 'I'm doing some very important research. Let Kalban handle this. I'll start being more involved next week. Or maybe next month, how does that sound? In the meanwhile, Kalban's going to take his Tests in two months. Let's look at this as a little ... preliminary trial.'

'But,' said Kalban, finally finding his voice, 'but I don't know enough about magic—and I'm not *nearly* strong enough to—do you have any idea what's happening in the city? Half the people think magic is unravelling. The Captain of the Guards says there might be a panic any moment. He says he's never seen anything like it—and this is a man who's spent the last forty years patrolling the streets of Madh. If Datta manages to harness public fear to support the Thoughtforms he and his associates create, there won't be *anything* anyone can do!'

Paras shrugged. 'Datta's monsters are monsters of the mind. You know it isn't a question of power. Even if it is, you have Meenakshi to help you, just like she did with the Illusion on the Academy. Someday you'll be ruling your own city. Melucha's problems tend more to aristocratic conspirators than rogue philosophers, I admit, but the principle is the same. You have to know how to deal with malcontents. You didn't *really* think I didn't know what was happening?'

'You've been scrying me,' Kalban accused.

'Of course I have. I'm not a total fool. I knew you were being secretive. I *expected* you to be secretive. You,' he said to Asamanjas, 'can stop worrying. It's better this way. Good practice for Meenakshi, too.'

'You're a raving lunatic,' groaned Asamanjas. 'That's the only explanation. You're a raving lunatic, and we're all going to die because of it.'

'Oh, calm down.' The amusement in Paras's voice made his brother's eyes blaze. He added to Kalban, 'I'll give you a note to take to Meenakshi.'

Kalban found Meenakshi and Chitralekha in the Academy library. Meenakshi was flicking through a book, while Chitralekha appeared to be amusing herself by making her scarves float in an imaginary breeze.

'Don't judge me,' she said, when she saw Kalban staring. 'It's not like I can help. I'm just here for moral support.'

He shook his head, sliding onto the bench next to Meenakshi and taking the next book from the stack.

'Avi isn't back, then?' he asked, passing Paras's note across. 'This is from your father.'

'No,' Chitralekha said as Meenakshi broke the seal with her thumb and unrolled the note. 'Maybe he's having a hard time finding Datta. I got the impression he wasn't in the Academy.'

'Can't you track him?' he asked Chitralekha.

'Not a practitioner and no magical ability to speak of, so I *can't* track him. The Inter-Realm Sensors can, but I'd have to go back and file a request and who knows how long *that* would take.'

'Don't you people have emergency protocols?'

'This isn't an emergency. Mortal Realm under threat because mortals are idiots and want to meddle in forces they can't control? We'll deal with it, yes, but by the time the paperwork goes through, Datta's little beasts could have levelled the city. No, anything we do is just us—and the Master Sorcerer?'

'No, he won't help.'

'Why not?'

'Because he's just like his daughter,' Kalban growled, making Meenakshi snicker.

'You're worrying too much,' she said. The sparkle in her

eyes would normally have sent Kalban straight to her study to investigate potential breaches of the Inter-Realm Code of Sorcery. 'There's always a solution. What's the worst-case scenario?'

'Five hundred rage monsters eat everyone in the city.'

'Fine, what's the *second*-worst-case scenario?'

'Meenakshi—'

'Look, the Thoughtforms might be powerful, but they're not here yet. Datta is and he's just a man.' Meenakshi crumpled the note and closed her fist around it. When she opened her fingers, it had been reduced to a pile of ash. 'A twisted man who wants to unleash forces he doesn't understand, yes, but still a mortal man. We can stop him. As soon as Avi's found him.'

'What was in the note?'

Meenakshi's face brightened. 'Everyone in the city is frightened, but not Datta. Not *yet*.'

Kalban fervently hoped that Paras hadn't made any suggestions about more griffons.

Before he could institute enquiries, Avi ran in. One of the guards from the Sun Temple was on his heels.

'My lord Kalban, I was sent to summon you to Temple Square at once.'

'Not now—'

'My lord, it is an emergency. You are needed.' The guard paused and shot a sideways glance at Meenakshi. 'You as well, my lady. If you please. My master bade me tell you ... A Mortal Realm portal has opened in Temple Square.'

'What!'

'That's what I meant to tell you,' gasped Avi. 'It's Datta.'

'He couldn't have done it,' protested Kalban. 'It takes power to open a portal.'

'The others helped him—the other members of the club. He said he could keep them out of trouble if they helped and they're afraid of being expelled without a Licence–'

'I doubt they'd be expelled,' said Kalban. 'They were misled by an authority figure, and no less than the Chair of a Department. That would be considered mitigating circumstances.'

'You try talking about mitigating circumstances to people who think their life's purpose is about to come to nothing! When the Thoughtform crossed into the Inter-Realm, it stopped drawing on their strength. That gave them an unexpected power surge. It took some time and effort, but they've just managed to open the portal.'

'But what's the point of a Mortal Realm portal?'

'He's gone to the Great Mountain of Ice for the phoenix. Manu told me—it's too late now, he'll bring it through any moment. There's nothing more to be done.'

'The *phoenix*?'

'That's *brilliant*,' breathed Meenakshi. Then, catching Kalban's eyes, she said, 'I'm sorry, it's terrible and evil and he ought to be ashamed of himself. But you have to admit it's brilliant. He needed the final piece of his puzzle, something to engender even more fear than seeing the Academy unmasked, enough fear for the spontaneous creation of Thoughtforms. What better than the first Thoughtform deliberately created?'

'Lecture later,' said Kalban. '*Come* now!'

CHAPTER XIX

Meenakshi had never ridden so hard in her life. She infinitely preferred walking—trotting on horseback made her feel ill—but, in typical fashion, the news that something strange and possibly dangerous was happening in Temple Square had spread. People in other cities might have begun fleeing in the opposite direction. Everyone in Madh, even in the current atmosphere of tension, was going to Temple Square to get a ringside seat.

All the same, there was something amiss. Normally the prospect of a good magical display would have had people hurrying there so eagerly it would have been impossible, even with four guards to clear the way, for horses to get through. Today, the crowd was thinner than usual.

Already, people were afraid.

Meenakshi saw Kalban shudder.

When they dismounted, they saw that a dozen Dismissers from the Dangerous Beings Control Squad had cleared the centre of the square and created a perimeter. That was all they'd managed to do. They were hard-pressed to hold the crowds back. They had no attention to spare for anything that might come through the portal.

The High Priest of the Sun God was standing within the cordon. Meenakshi was impressed. Divine intercessor he might be, but he would be powerless in the current situation, and he was smart enough to know it. He stood there all the same, the head of his staff catching the light from the lamps around the square and shining like a tiny sun. His jaw was set and no visible emotion showed on his face.

Through the portal, on the other side, Meenakshi could see a sloping field of ice and snow flurrying in the blustering wind.

And she could *hear* a screech higher and eerier than the wind howling on a winter's night. None of her griffons sounded like that.

'Can you do anything to it?' she asked Chitralekha. 'Tame it?'

'My powers only work on naturally born creatures, or your griffon would have been eating out of my hand by now.'

'It's not Alchemy. It's a Thoughtform! It comes from the human mind. Your powers work on the mind, don't they?'

'I could try,' said Chitralekha doubtfully. 'It might be easier than the Hidden Man in the Academy, since there were only two minds involved in creating the phoenix. But one of them was the Fifth High Loremaster—he was particularly stubborn. I don't know!'

Meenakshi slipped through the cordon, Kalban and Chitralekha behind her. Avi had melted into the panicked crowd, doubtless adding to their terror with his own, but there was no time to worry about him.

'We're trying to hold it back!' shouted the nearest Dismisser. 'But it's too strong.'

'Let it through,' said Meenakshi. 'You can't throw brute force against it. It won't work. Let it through. We'll see what happens.'

The High Priest of the Sun God glanced at her. 'With all due respect, my lady, are you sure you can handle whatever comes through the portal?'

Meenakshi smiled. 'Not at all.'

The High Priest stared at her for what seemed like an eternity. Meenakshi's opinion of him rose further when, with a visible effort of will, he lowered his staff.

'Have at it,' he said. 'If we're meant to see the dawn, you'll find a way.'

The phoenix came through the portal in a blaze of light so bright Meenakshi almost missed the man who stumbled after it.

Nobody else noticed him at all. He stood behind the phoenix, his eyes narrowed with concentration. Meenakshi felt something that was at once powerful and alien, a strength of will and purpose that, although it had no hint of magic, was almost— *almost*—enough to control the creature.

For a moment, she felt sorry for him. If not for that long-ago incident, one that most young sorcerers would have put behind them after exacting suitable vengeance in the form of a swarm of bees or a winged camel, Datta might have been so much more than a man skulking in the shadows, using his students to support his foredoomed attempt to settle a grudge.

And, thanks to her father's information, Datta's attempt *was* foredoomed.

Animals, much like humans, couldn't be entirely controlled by magic. Nevertheless, it was possible for someone with sufficient skill to amplify and direct their inborn instincts.

Swans are among the most aggressive of the winged beasts, particularly in defence of their territory. Several of those that inhabited the city were already flying in to investigate the intruder. It didn't take much effort for Meenakshi to channel their anger to the man controlling the phoenix, rather than the phoenix itself.

Datta was so intent on his task that he didn't hear their hissing or the flapping of their wings until they were almost upon him. Then he screamed and dived for the cover of the nearest statue. His hold on the phoenix unravelled.

'Get him!' Meenakshi shouted to Kalban.

She didn't have time to see if he had heard. Her attention was riveted by the phoenix.

Meenakshi had never seen one before. Even she drew the line at having a phoenix inside the city.

It was surprisingly small, hardly larger than a rooster. Its plumage was black, its eyes glowing like embers amidst its feathers. They were the only part of it that looked dangerous.

It squawked, a surprisingly discordant note. The cobbles under its talons began to smoulder.

'Do something!' Meenakshi told Chitralekha.

'I can't—fine, I'll try.' She took a step towards the phoenix, holding out a hand as you might to a pet a cat or a mynah bird. 'Good phoenix. Want a cracker?' She turned back to Meenakshi. 'You can conjure crackers, right?'

'I don't think it wants crackers!'

The tip of the God of Watchful Peace's spear caught fire.

'No,' Kalban whispered. 'No, no, no, this is bad.'

'We can replace the spear!'

'Look *around*, Meenakshi.'

Meenakshi looked. Despite the seriousness of the situation, she couldn't help admiring the thoroughness of Datta's planning. He had been laying the groundwork for days, perhaps weeks. He and his students had begun the process, drawing on the fear thrumming through the gathered crowd to create Thoughtforms. As the fires blazed in Temple Square, that fear began to craft their physical forms.

All around the square, over the heads of the crowd, shapes of mist were coalescing, dissipating and reforming. They were monstrous, winged and clawed and fanged, illustrations from a bestiary brought to life. It was what people believed about the phoenix, Meenakshi realised; none of them had seen it.

Terrifying as the shapes were, they were ephemeral, none lasting more than a few seconds.

More and more fires were catching all around the square now. Every time another one blazed to life, Meenakshi felt a tug on reality as the Thoughtforms gained a shred of power.

'Stop the fires!' snapped Chitralekha. 'They're making it worse.'

Meenakshi turned, but the High Priest shook his head. 'I'm on it. Fires, I can handle. And I see the Arcane Zoology Authorisation Desk has just arrived. I'll tell them to round up the swans. You worry about *that* thing. And all those *other* things. And later,' he added, as he ran in the direction of the Sun Temple with a turn of speed Meenakshi would never have expected of a man in ankle-length robes, 'I want an explanation!'

His departure was followed by the arrival of the Captain of the City Guard. He took in the scene at a glance—you didn't get to be Captain of the City Guard in Madh by being slow on the uptake—

and looked from Kalban to Meenakshi.

'What should we do?'

His voice was even, with no hint of panic, screaming or pleading for his life.

'Hold the crowd,' said Kalban. 'You can't help us, but maybe you can free up some of the Dismissers. And get that man somewhere other than here.' He indicated Datta, who was struggling in the grip of two junior priests. 'Chitralekha, can you do *anything*?'

'Don't you think I would have by now?' Chitralekha said angrily, pulling off a scarf whose fringe had started smoking. 'This thing is immune to anything I can do.'

'Not about the phoenix,' bellowed Kalban. 'About the people panicking and making *more* monsters we'll have to deal with.'

'Oh! That! Yes. But Section XV of the Inter-Realm Accord—'

'Meenakshi, give her permission! And douse the phoenix!'

Meenakshi gave permission with a nod. Dousing the phoenix was harder. She tried all the usual methods—water, sand, a little blast of frigid air—but nothing worked. The water turned to steam, the sand to a shower of translucent crystals that fell to the ground and would have had people scrambling to grab them if they hadn't been under the red-hot claws of a magical bird, and the frigid air had no effect at all. It probably reminded the phoenix of its home.

The portal was still open. Meenakshi considered just pushing the phoenix back through it. She could do it, if she could get just a step closer—

'Don't!' shouted Kalban, reading her mind. 'That won't make them any less afraid of it.'

'Then what do you suggest?'

'Put it out!'

Vacuum, Meenakshi thought for a moment. The phoenix couldn't burn if it had nothing to burn. But, no, she didn't actually want to harm it. It was only following its instincts, after all. It wasn't the phoenix's fault that the Fifth High Loremaster had made it or that Datta had dragged it from its comfortable home into a city square full of screaming people. That would be enough to put anyone in a bad mood.

Experimentally, she pulled out the air in a bubble around it, leaving it enough to breathe, just as she did when she wanted to avoid eavesdroppers.

The phoenix's raucous cries went abruptly silent, but fires were still blazing all around her.

The High Priest reemerged from the Sun Temple, followed by a line of junior priests and guards carrying buckets. Water might not work on the phoenix, but it did work on the pilings, scarves and other assorted scraps that were catching fire.

Meenakshi ignored the people hurrying around the square dousing fires until someone threw a bucket on the phoenix. It hissed into steam before it got near it.

'Nope,' muttered Meenakshi, letting the vacuum dissipate. 'How are we doing on the Thoughtforms?'

'Better,' said Kalban, but the tense edge in his voice belied his words. 'Chitralekha's *good*. We may have ten *minutes* now instead of ten seconds. Don't worry about the Thoughtforms, Meenakshi. Find a way to put the bird out! Then they'll *see* there's nothing to fear.'

'That's ridiculous!' protested the High Priest. 'It'll have the opposite of the effect you intend.'

'What are you talking about?'

'Wasn't it some Meluchan philosopher who said people worship what they fear? I know how crowds work, Kalban, especially terrified crowds. I have no idea why you want them to feel like there's nothing to be afraid of.' He stepped back to allow an acolyte with a basin to scamper past him. 'Personally, I think fear is the most appropriate response in the current situation. It shows good judgement. But if you want them to stop being afraid, proving that the Master Sorcerer's daughter is powerful isn't the answer. They know that already. It won't make them any less frightened of the phoenix.'

'You're right,' Kalban muttered. 'But what would make them not be afraid?'

'There you have me. I don't know anything about phoenixes. Maybe if it turns out to be a turtle dove in disguise?'

'I doubt that's going to happen. Meenakshi, you've done the research. Phoenixes. Behaviour. What do you know?'

'I just know the stories—'

'The same stories the Fifth High Loremaster knew! What are they?'

'Is this any time for a lesson in Arcane Zoology?' came Chitralekha's voice. 'I can't hold a crowd like this forever. One of you hurry up and do something!'

'Meenakshi,' Kalban urged. 'The phoenix.'

'It bursts into flame and is reborn. That's all there is.' Meenakshi put out a fire on the pedestal of the Goddess of Speech.

'What about setting everything else on fire? How is it doing that?'

'Spillover from the magic it generates when it's close to immolating itself.' The High Priest groaned. 'That's all there *is*, Kalban. There's nothing about how to stop it. The legends say you *can't*.'

'Does anybody know why it's choosing to burst into flames *now*?'

'Stress, I suppose. This can't be pleasant. It isn't bursting into flames yet, though. It's just ... getting close to it. When it's a few hours from bursting into flame, everything will be burning from the spillover. Of course, it stops once the phoenix has caught fire. We're probably a day away from that. At least.'

'Small mercies,' said the High Priest.

But Kalban had a peculiar look in his eye. 'What makes it immolate itself?'

'Old age. Danger. Like a lizard losing its tail.'

'Do it.'

'*What?*' demanded Meenakshi, at the same moment as the High Priest yelled, 'Are you *insane*?' and Chitralekha enquired if Kalban was suffering ill effects from the heat.

'Give it danger,' Kalban repeated. 'Make it burn. *Quickly*.'

'You'll kill us all!' protested the High Priest.

'No, she won't. Not if she's quick. Throw *everything* you have at it, Meenakshi. Scare it enough and it'll start burning at once. Magical spillover normally takes a couple of seconds to take effect—'

'And if the spillover stops by then, nothing will burn.'

'Do it,' repeated Kalban. 'Nothing happens once it's reborn, right? The phoenix isn't a threat?'

'No, it's supposed to be friendliest in the immediate aftermath of a rebirth.'

'You think that'll make people stop being afraid?' Kalban asked the High Priest.

'Bring about the thing they fear most and prove that it didn't harm them? If anything could work ...'

'Fine.' Kalban stepped up behind Meenakshi. 'Don't worry about the spillover. I'll take care of it. You just throw every bit of power at the phoenix.'

Meenakshi sent a small, experimental jolt in the phoenix's direction. It squawked and scrambled back. The air grew just a fraction warmer.

'Hurry,' said Kalban. 'We're running out of time on the Thoughtforms.'

Meenakshi drew a deep breath and flung all her power into a bolt of magical energy directed at the phoenix.

The stones around it started to glow. The air grew hot. For a moment, she thought it hadn't been enough, or not quick enough. A misty haze descended on the square.

The phoenix burst into flame.

It seemed like the phoenix's fire sucked all the heat from its surroundings, because every other fire in the square went out at once. Bizarrely, it felt as if there was a definite chill in the air.

The phoenix burned in a flash, and there was a little pile of ashes on the blackened cobbles. Before Meenakshi could do more than take a step forward, the air over the ashes began to sparkle. The ground seemed to melt. Up rose the phoenix, black as the night, but it was different now. Friendlier, just like the books said. There was no threat in its glowing eyes.

Its discordant squawk was milder.

'Go back,' said Meenakshi, indicating the portal through which, now that the fires had been doused, she could feel icy blasts of air. 'Go home.'

The phoenix cocked its head and studied her for a long moment.

Then it turned and went.

Around the square, Meenakshi felt the Thoughtforms dissipate.

EPILOGUE

'Guess who's the newest Class III Celestial Dancer!'

Kalban looked up from his book. 'How did you get in?'

'Don't worry, I filled the paperwork. All ninety-three million pages of it. I brought a copy of the authorisation, too.' Chitralekha thrust a stamped form at him before sitting beside Meenakshi. 'There's less now that I'm Class III. I don't need to name a specific target, for one thing.'

'Good for you,' Meenakshi said, turning a page.

Chitralekha lifted an eyebrow. 'Now *he* I can believe is studying for Finals. I'm glad to see you took my advice, by the way, Kalban. What are *you* doing in the Governor's Library on a day when you could be outside letting the griffon stretch his wings? What are you calling it, anyway?'

'His name's Griffon.'

'That's unoriginal.'

'But accurate.' Meenakshi shrugged. 'Anyway, he responds to it.'

'He responds to *you*,' Kalban corrected. 'And if you want to know what Meenakshi is doing, she's sitting there pretending to be studying Mathematics and imagining I don't know she has a Bestiary of the Arcane open under the table.'

Chitralekha reached under the table for the book, shut it, and put it back in Meenakshi's hands. 'Read later. Talk to me now. Where's Kalban's crazy friend?'

'He's not crazy,' Kalban said. 'He's gone back to Melucha.'

'I thought the Master Sorcerer and the Master of the Academy agreed not to expel the students involved.'

'The Master Sorcerer wanted to put them all on phoenix-feeding duty. That would have been making the punishment fit the crime, but the Student Council intervened on their behalf. They're going to be spending their free time over the next six months at the Arcane Zoology Authorisation Desk, taking care of all the animals that get confiscated for being too dangerous to be at large.' Kalban shrugged. 'I don't think Avi could face the idea. I suppose he'll apply for his license in Melucha.'

'He was feeling trapped in Madh,' said Chitralekha. 'Datta knew that.'

'Why didn't any of them suspect something?' Meenakshi asked. 'Did they really think it was just a thought exercise? That's unlikely.'

'Datta heard his students argue about Ethics so much, he must have known them very well. He knew enough to know how to persuade them to try. The danger would have been no deterrent to students of the Academy. If any of them *did* realise what they were creating... well, by then it was probably too late.'

'Who would have thought Avi would be the one with the courage to tell someone?'

'It's lucky he's Kalban's friend, or he mightn't have dared ... We might never know for certain, but I wouldn't be surprised if Datta gave him a little nudge in that direction. Datta didn't want to be *seen* to be asking for help, but he did want someone—preferably the Master Sorcerer, but he was willing to settle for Meenakshi—to try. The Free Bow who tried to get into Meenakshi's apartments was told to leave an anonymous note about what was happening. I spoke to Datta,' Chitralekha added, in response to Kalban's questioning look.

'Your request was approved? Good for you. I suppose your promotion made it easier. What else did he tell you?'

'His plans seem to have been more elaborate than I gave him credit for. We did our part, playing into his hands,' she added ruefully. 'I should have known it was Datta as soon as I saw him. I sensed the anger in him, but I didn't think about it. I assumed he was frustrated with his students.'

'You didn't know about his old feud with the Master Sorcerer?'

Chitralekha looked embarrassed. 'That swan incident *was* in the records. But it's not unusual for students of sorcery to play pranks on each other. You have no idea what a field day the Sprites have had over this. They're insisting that none of *them* would have overlooked the possibility of unresolved childhood enmity.'

'I think,' replied Kalban, choosing his words carefully, 'that Datta felt as humiliated as he did, and bore the grudge so long, precisely because he *wasn't* a student of sorcery. A little ... discretion ... on the part of the Master Sorcerer might have prevented it.'

'You can stop looking at me sidelong,' said Meenakshi. 'I *know* it isn't unreasonable provocation if someone disturbs me while I'm reading.'

'Good. Now if you can avoid getting into a blood feud with Clever Raman, Madh may not have a repeat of this incident in thirty years.'

'In any case,' Chitralekha put in, 'Datta could never have been content in Madh. He wanted power, but this isn't a city he or anyone can put in order. There's too much magic and too much traffic between the Realms.'

'He managed to use that to his advantage,' said Kalban. 'Black Sands. The Lake Guardian. *They* must have known he couldn't want the Nectar for any good purpose.'

'They'll be dealt with. It's not unusual for gods whose cults come close to dying to take drastic measures. They were both powerful gods in their time. It's a little sad, if you think about it. Five hundred years ago, if they'd been frustrated they would have been saying it with hellfire and flash floods. Now they've been reduced to smuggling Nectar across the Inter-Realm border for a megalomaniac who was doomed to fail.'

'Doomed to fail?' asked Meenakshi. 'He nearly succeeded.'

'The Thoughtforms weren't his purpose. He wanted power. He thought he could control them, and, through them, the city. Maybe he even had more extensive ambitions.'

'He was a fool if he thought he could control them.'

'He was an intelligent man,' said Kalban. 'A fool couldn't have gone as far as dragging the phoenix into Temple Square. He made the mistake of overestimating his own capabilities. He wouldn't be the first.'

'The phoenix was frightened,' Meenakshi mused. 'It just wanted to go home.'

'You're right about that,' said Chitralekha. 'I can't be certain, but I'd guess that none of them—none of the little group that made that first Thoughtform—really wanted to be here. They're good enough with magic to be at the Academy, but not good enough to do very much. It got them worrying that they couldn't do *anything*. I still don't understand what that had to do with the cloaking spell on the Academy, though.'

'Illusions are easy,' said Meenakshi. 'They replace reality with a bit of something taken from your own mind. Something you're expecting to see, so you don't ask too many questions about it. But the Illusion on the Academy is different. It was meant to strike a little ... awe, maybe, or fear ... into people. But that comes from the fear of the magicians who built it. It wouldn't make the study of magic any less interesting to do it in a normal building that doesn't have moss growing up half the walls.'

'Just like the people who made the Thoughtform were afraid.'

'It was the same fear,' said Kalban. 'The fear of not being recognised as extraordinary. And it came because they were all forcing themselves to do this, to be here, because they thought magical power was special.'

'But it's not.' Meenakshi snapped her fingers, setting a little bookend in the shape of a milkmaid dancing in a crooked jig across the table. 'Magic's like ... I don't know, like gravity. It just *is*. You can't be frightened of it. You can't *want* it. That's when it gets away from you. It was really the same solution both times ... Admitting the truth.'

'Truth can be frightening.'

'Not as frightening as fear of it.'

'I think Avi's happy now,' Kalban offered. 'He doesn't have to pretend he cares about Alchemy anymore. He might even find out what he *does* care about.'

'Maybe.' Chitralekha watched the dancing milkmaid until Meenakshi stopped its movement with another snap of her fingers. 'Anyway, I thought you might be interested in knowing about the Thoughtform. Urvashi and Rambha both spoke to him. They're not quite sure what he *can* do. But he came from fear, so for now they've classed him Dangerous to Mortals. That means no independent Mortal Realm Pass and no crossing the border without a chaperone and an invitation.'

'He can't be Summoned?'

'Were you planning on trying?'

'No.'

'Good. For as much as it's worth, he can't be Summoned.' Chitralekha got to her feet. 'All right, then. Kalban, you get back to your studying. Meenakshi, you get back to ... whatever you're planning to do with that book. I'll be in touch.'

She had vanished before Kalban could say, 'Please don't.'

He looked over the top of his Rhetoric textbook at Meenakshi. 'That's that. We know everything.'

'Don't be ridiculous.' She favoured Kalban with a roll of the eyes that was oddly reminiscent of his mother. 'There's one thing we don't know—and that's something you, at least, *should* know.'

'What's that?'

'Why didn't you want to tell Father?'

Kalban felt a little unpleasant shock. He hadn't realised he'd been hoping to avoid that question until Meenakshi asked it. 'Avi asked for my help. You know that. You don't think I had anything to do with what they were doing?'

'Don't be stupid. You barely even like legitimate Alchemy. Why would I suspect you of dabbling in arcane, proscribed forms of magic? That's why it makes no sense.'

'Anytime you feel like explaining, Meenakshi.'

'I would have expected you to go running to Father or the Master of the Academy as soon as we had reason to suspect it might be more than your crazy friend's hallucinations. And, at the very least, I would have expected you to insist on Chitralekha leaving for good. But you let her help. And you didn't tell Father until the time he would have had to know anyway. Why?'

'You noticed that I didn't tell him. And you don't know why?'

'If I knew, I wouldn't ask.'

Kalban thought of the past few days, of Avi, of Chitralekha, and of Paras's calm insistence on his taking his Tests. He thought of the courtiers of Melucha, eyeing him with questions that they were too polite to put into words.

'I haven't answered my brother's letter yet. Some day I'll be Prince Regnant of Melucha.'

'Some day before that you'll be a licensed sorcerer. What's your point?'

'Nothing. I'm just glad I'll never be Master Sorcerer.'

And, he thought, although he did not say, that he was glad Meenakshi was Meenakshi. In the wrong hands, a desperate desire to be well-regarded could do far worse damage than detached goodwill.

'If you say so.' Meenakshi returned to her book.

'Yes.' Kalban paused. 'Can I borrow your *Alchemical Bestiary*? I have Tests to prepare for.'

A REPRESENTATION OF THE GOVERNANCE STRUCTURE AND ASSOCIATED DEPARTMENTS IN THE CITY OF MADH

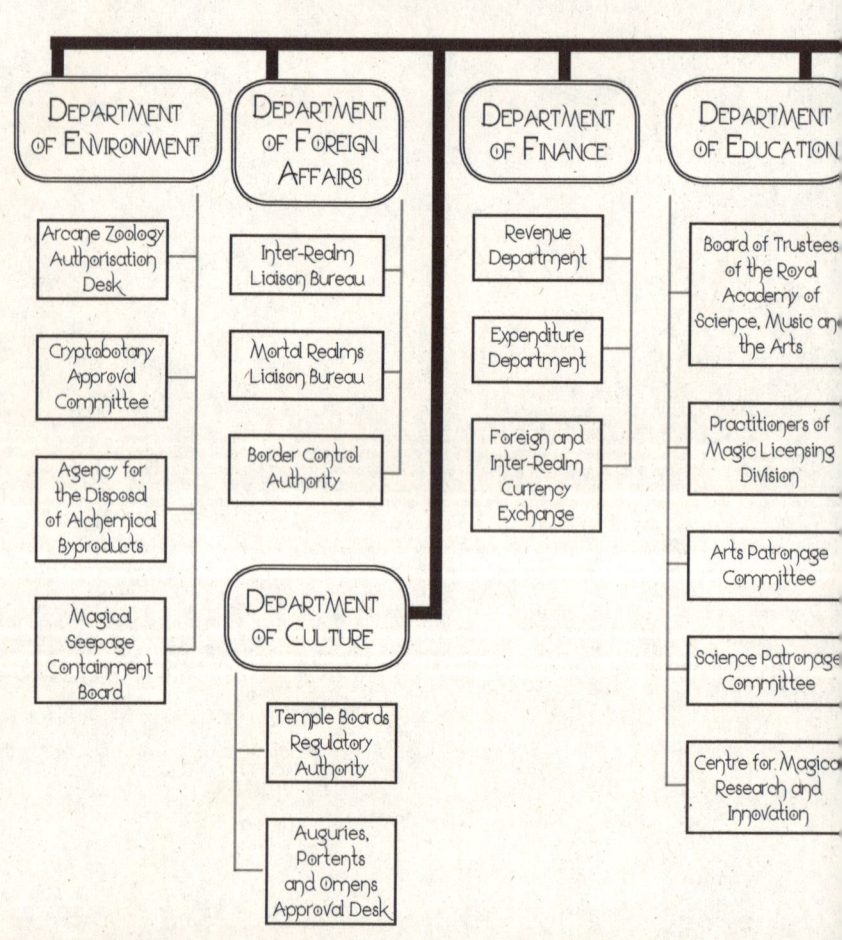

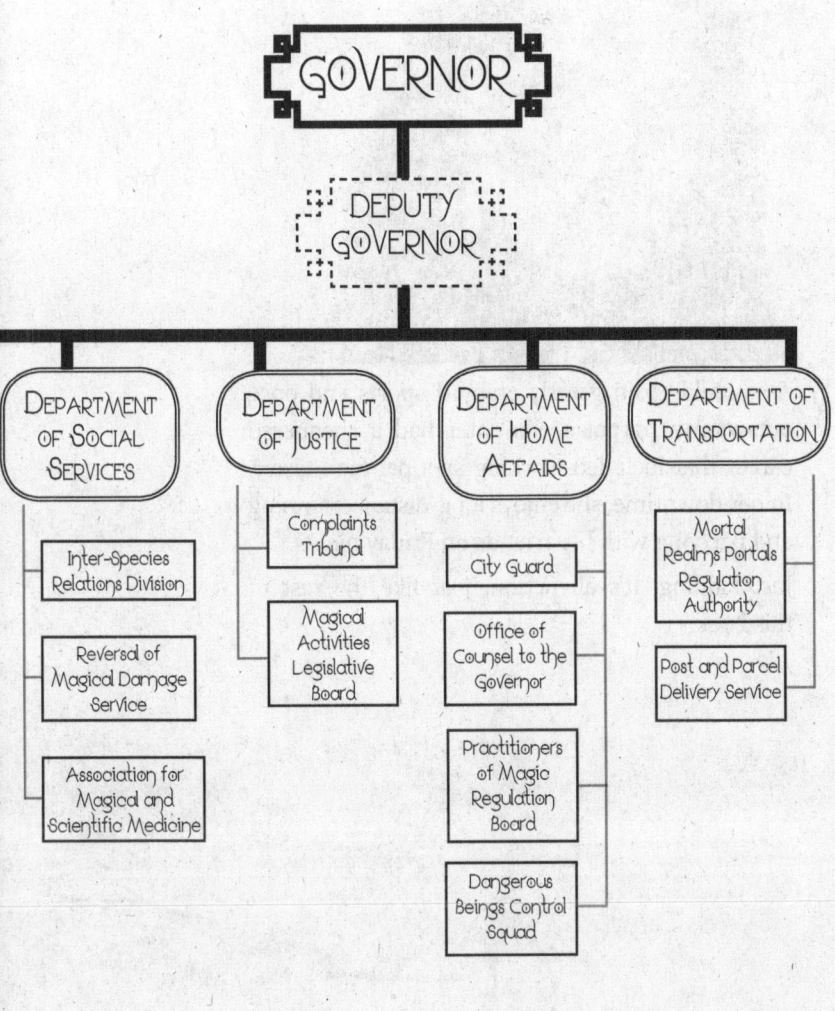

As a child, Aditi greatly enjoyed sports and once outswam a porpoise. She later had a chequered career that included working as a pet food taster. In her downtime, she enjoys long-distance running and partying with her friends on Friday nights.

Just kidding. It's all fiction, just like the rest of this book.